"You know you want to stay with me."

Even as Ellis denied Steve's statement, she knew it was true. She was in love with him, and she wanted to stay with him forever. Oh, why hadn't she agreed to Steve's original proposition? Why hadn't she taken a chance and married him?

Now it was too late. Jan, his glamorous ex-fiancée, was planning to come back to him. And, unlike Ellis, Jan would give him what he wanted, with or without an engagement ring; with or without love.

"I could persuade you to stay, Ellis," Steve continued. "I could give you everything you desire."

Everything, Ellis thought bitterly, but his love! "I'm sorry, Steve," she said slowly. "I'm going home."

OTHER
Harlequin Romances
by DOROTHY CORK

Island
of Escape

by

DOROTHY CORK

Harlequin Books

TORONTO • LONDON • NEW YORK • AMSTERDAM
SYDNEY • HAMBURG • PARIS

Original hardcover edition published in 1978
by Mills & Boon Limited

ISBN 0-373-02259-X

Harlequin edition published May 1979

CHAPTER ONE

ELLIS scarcely recognised herself in the girl who looked back at her from the mirror in the hotel bedroom, high above Sandy Bay. She couldn't help thinking that if she had looked like this just two weeks ago, then Paul might not have ditched her and been so easily diverted by Jan's charms. She had grown used to that sort of thing happening, of course. Men rarely looked again at Ellis Lincoln once they had met her volatile and beautiful cousin Jan.

But this time was different. Paul was the first man she had really felt seriously about, and Jan had broken up the affair so easily.

Ellis leaned closer to her reflection to smooth colour over her lips, and had to blink away tears from her eyes even as she took in, with a new shock of surprise, her changed appearance. The light golden-brown hair, which she always used to wear long and neatly drawn back from her face, had been cut short and completely restyled, and she had been shown by an expert how to use, to full effect, the expensive make-up that Jake had insisted she should buy. Tonight, her darkly lashed blue eyes looked like jewels in their setting of subtly applied eye-shadow, and as if all this were not enough, she wore the most sophisticated and beautiful dress she had ever owned in all her twenty years. It was a blue and green affair of finest voile, the halter-neck, that showed off her smooth young shoulders, looped through with a wide band of fine gold mesh, fastened at one side by a sparkling clasp. She had, in fact, become such a stranger to herself that she found it hard to reconcile what she saw with what she knew herself to be—a quiet, almost plain girl, very unsophisticated, and completely lacking in charisma, as Jan had remarked once. A girl who kept house for her uncle in a Melbourne suburb.

Well, all that had come to an end since Jan had come home from Flinders Island and annexed Paul Howard. Ellis simply couldn't stay there any longer, and though she did it reluctantly, she left her uncle in Jan's decidedly unwilling hands and flew across Bass Strait to spend a week in Hobart with Jake Armour.

'The best way to mend a broken heart,' Jake claimed, 'is to go somewhere different—meet new people— enjoy yourself,' and he had written Ellis a bracing letter. 'Come to Hobart and join me at the Casino Hotel. You'll have the whale of a time—you'll soon forget that fellow. He can't be worth breaking your heart over anyhow, if he prefers that minx Jan to you. I never did like that girl. I remember saying to Siddie when we left you with the Websters, That young miss will eat little Ellis alive——'

Jake had been Ellis's father's closest friend, and when Ellis was orphaned at eleven, she had spent three years—three happy years—with him and his wife, Siddie. Then he had gone broke, completely broke, and reluctantly passed her over to her aunt and uncle, who had looked after her and educated her. Ellis had barely left school and started work in a bank when her aunt died, and since Jan, despite being two years older than Ellis, was too giddy and irresponsible to be trusted, it was Ellis who took over the housekeeping for her uncle and for Jan and Martin. It was not long after that that Siddie and Jake came into a small fortune and wanted her to come back to them, but out of loyalty and gratitude she stayed with her uncle.

And now she would never go back. She had made up her mind . . .

Ellis glanced at the little jewelled watch on her wrist. It was time to go downstairs. If Jake had had enough of the gaming tables in the main casino, he would be waiting for her. They were going to dine in the Cabaret Room and then watch the show, and Ellis had a slight feeling of trepidation, because Jake was pressing her to go back to Adelaide with him and be the daughter he had never had. Siddie had died over two years ago, and now he was going to marry again and Ellis knew, though it didn't seem to have occurred to Jake, that it would be a great mistake for him to present his new wife with an unknown, twenty-year-old 'daughter'. She could only hope and pray that she would hear soon about the position she had applied for on Flinders Island.

Taking up her evening purse, she made her way to the elevator. She was sure she would be happy working on a sheep farm—or a sheep station, as Jan called it. She would feel herself useful, she would be busy, and in time, she supposed, she would get over Paul. Time, people said, was a great healer when it came to all sorts of ills, including broken hearts.

Travelling down in the lift among a crowd of well-dressed chattering people, Ellis wondered just why she hadn't heard from Steve Gascoyne in answer to her letter. Perhaps he didn't want to have any dealings with a cousin of Jan's. The very thought of how Jan had treated him troubled Ellis's conscience, as so many of the things Jan did troubled her conscience. Like not staying in to answer the phone when she had promised her father she would, or going out for the day with her latest boy-friend instead of typing out the letters her father paid her to deal with. Ellis didn't know how many times she herself had stayed up till all hours of the night doing Jan's typing for her—and getting no thanks for it. She didn't know, either, how many lies she had told on her cousin's behalf when Jan had capriciously decided to 'forget' a date.

And now there was Steve Gascoyne, this poor sheep farmer whom Jan had actually promised to marry. Ellis felt so sorry for him! She pictured him as a nice unsophisticated countryman who probably could hardly believe that anyone like Jan could have fallen in love with him. And then Jan, no more than three days after she came home to Melbourne, rather obviously decided that Paul Howard, a young and successful real estate developer, was more to her taste. To give her her due, Ellis thought she was genuinely unaware that Paul had been *her* property till then, because a man as eligible as Paul was very hard to associate with a girl like Ellis.

Ellis stepped out of the elevator and crossed the foyer towards the main casino, her eyes suddenly filling with the tears that would come when she thought of Paul. He had been so nice to her—he had taken her to a show, come to dinner, talked to her about all sorts of fascinating things.

And he had kissed her.

Oh, how she had fantasised about him—when she lay in bed at night, and at all hours of the day. It had been an effort to keep him out of her mind as she did her uncle's typing for him. She had taken *that* on so Jan could have a holiday with her brother Martin, a naturalist, who was doing research on various birds on Flinders Island. Ellis had thought it odd that Jan should be interested in going to such a small out-of-the-way place, but in no time she had plunged into a love affair with Steve Gascoyne. 'A *torrid* love affair,' she had written, and her letters had been full of satisfaction.

Now the engagement was off. The ring, a very beautiful one, had been returned by registered post. Exactly why was a mystery to Ellis. She was inclined to suspect that Jan had been rather cruelly amusing herself by having a 'torrid' love affair with a simple farmer. One thing that was plain was that she had left the island when she did because she didn't want to let herself in for any household chores.

'Steve's aunt was taken off to hospital in Hobart by the Flying Doctor Service,' she had told Ellis. 'And I have a very nasty feeling she won't be coming back. Which does rather make one think, seeing that she did all the housekeeping. I really couldn't see myself taking that on—and certainly not cooking for the shearers when that comes around.'

But was that a good enough reason for breaking an engagement if you really loved a man? Ellis wouldn't have thought so. Still, Jan had always been fickle—and she was so attractive to the opposite sex she could pick and choose all she liked.

And now she had chosen Paul.

Ellis swallowed back her tears as she moved towards the Cabaret Room, and stood still for a moment glancing around her. The golden cages at the mini dice spun, the big dice tumbled. The croupier at one of the roulette tables raked in the chips, and from another came the call, *'Faites vos jeux!'* Dealers at the blackjack tables, vivid in their vermilion dresses, flipped cards from the 'shoe', and from their high chairs the inspectors, formal in black suits and white shirts, presided over each game.

The place teemed with people—tourists and locals

and gamblers, among them many Asiatics from the boats that were in the harbour, and Ellis, failing to see Jake, pressed on towards their meeting place. He wasn't there, and a little uncertainly she took a chair at a small table not far from the bar, and hoped that he would turn up soon. She was not used to such sophistication—her life in Melbourne had been quiet in the extreme—and she hoped that in this dimly lit part of the casino she wouldn't attract attention.

But before very long she became aware that a man was studying her. She could feel his eyes roving over her, and she shrank within herself, wishing she could suddenly become invisible. Then unexpectedly her confusion gave way to a completely different feeling as she realised she was no longer the neatly dressed little innocent who had kept house in a Melbourne suburb. She remembered the image she had seen in the mirror——

Unable to resist it, she glanced across at the man who was taking such an interest in her, and she did it boldly and openly. He too was alone at a small table, but he had a glass of something—probably Scotch, she decided—in his hand. She judged him to be somewhere in his mid-thirties, for though his thick dark hair had a dramatic silver streak in it, his deeply tanned and strikingly handsome face was young. He wore a velvet jacket of darkest brown, a pale peach-coloured shirt and a silky, striped tie, and as he moved one arm she caught the flash of gold cuff links.

Their eyes met, and, without altogether meaning to she smiled, then felt her heart give a nervous leap as he smiled back and raised his glass to her. There was a very decidedly worldly cynicism in his smile, and she looked away hastily, aware that he might think she was inviting him to pick her up. She opened her purse and pretended to hunt for something in it, and hoped he wouldn't come over and speak to her. She'd have no idea what to say to a man like that. He belonged to a world that was completely different from hers— though, seeing her in this get-up, that fact wouldn't be so apparent to him, she thought wryly.

She had an almost irresistible compulsion to look at him again—aloofly, haughtily, this time, just to show that she wasn't in the least interested in him, but probably fortunately for her, Jake arrived—handsome, suave, with nothing of the father figure about him, despite his fifty-one years. Wealth, Ellis thought irrelevantly, certainly suited him, and she smiled at him affectionately.

He greeted her as gallantly as if she were some woman he was interested in romantically, instead of just Ellis Lincoln, whom he'd known since she was a small child.

'My darling, you look beautiful. That new hairstyle couldn't suit you better.'

As he spoke, he raised her hand to his lips and kissed her fingertips. It was all part of his policy of making her feel better, of boosting up her ego, and though she knew he did it to make her feel good, she was aware that people looked and smiled cynically—just as that man in the velvet jacket was looking now. And she had a pretty fair idea as to what he was thinking.

'I'm sorry I've kept you waiting,' Jake was saying. 'You should have bought yourself a drink ... I had a real run of luck at roulette just now, and I didn't want to get out too soon. Forgive me? Anyhow, let's eat, shall we?'

Ellis nodded and got to her feet and let Jake take her arm. Deliberately, she didn't glance at the man who had been staring at her, as they went into the Cabaret

Room, and she told herself firmly she simply didn't care *what* he thought.

Jake ordered pre-dinner drinks when they were seated at their table, then once he had decided what they'd have for dinner, he produced a small packet from his pocket and handed it across the table to Ellis.

'Here's something I picked up in Battery Point while you were at the hairdresser's today. See if you like it.'

Oh dear! Ellis felt slightly embarrassed, though she knew Jake hated her to feel that way. He had heaped so many gifts on her, and her pale cheeks flushed as she thanked him and opened the packet to discover it contained a little gold bracelet, set with small sapphires.

'Jake, it's beautiful! But you really shouldn't——'

As she spoke, a man came down the shallow steps and paused nearby, waiting to be shown to his table. It was, Ellis noticed with an inward glance, that man with the silver-streaked hair, and as she glanced at him, it was obvious from the derisive lift at the corners of his rather wide and sensual mouth, that he had noticed what was going on at her table. She looked way from him angrily, disliking him intensely. He took it for granted, of course, that she was accepting jewellery from an older man in return for favours given or hoped for. He wouldn't for an instant see Jake as a kindly uncle or a godfather—not after the way he had kissed her fingers earlier on. She was thankful when the waiter came and he was taken to a table that, though it was within sight, was at least out of earshot!

Jake had taken the bracelet and was fastening it round her wrist.

'No protests, darling. Giving you things is my pleasure. Having money is no use unless you have someone to share it with, and Siddie and I had precious little time.' He didn't release her wrist, but looked at her seriously. 'Am I going to be able to persuade you to forget about this job you've applied for and come to live with me and Pat? You'll get along very well together, I promise you.'

Ellis bit her lip and awkwardly moved her hand from his to pick up her glass.

'Jake, I—I don't know what to say. I feel so ungrateful, but the fact is, I just don't think I could adjust to doing nothing. I know you think I'm mad to have applied for a position as housekeeper, but it's really what I want. I want to be independent, to—to do some kind of work——'

He frowned thoughtfully. 'But not *that* kind of work, Ellis. I don't know how you came to apply for such a position, but as far as I can see it will be a case of jumping out of the frying pan into the fire. You'll be a drudge. It's just not good enough. You've slaved for that uncle of yours for long enough while Jan's messed around enjoying herself, and you'd be wasting yourself to go off and do the same thing for some sheep farmer. When I think what a pathetic, unhappy little thing you looked the day I met you at the airport last week, and how in just a few days you've blossomed out into a beauty—a real beauty—I regret the years you've been away from me.' He paused and gave her a long look. 'Didn't you see yourself in the glass before you came downstairs tonight? There's not a woman in this room can hold a candle to you. You're a—a mad mixture of sophistication and innocence, of lady and coquette. You'd have a wonderful life with Pat and me —you'd meet all sorts of eligible fellows, forget that idiot Paul completely——'

Ellis shook her head hopelessly. It would be impossible to tell him that Pat wouldn't really want her, and after a second she said ruefully, 'I guess there's something wrong with me, then, Jake, because most of all I want to do something useful—I really do. And—and I'm not a beauty. You've given me some lovely clothes, I've learnt how to make the most of myself, and I know I look a lot nicer than I did, but inside I'm just Ellis Lincoln.' She sighed a little. 'I really would like to get this job I've applied for. Besides, isn't work supposed to be an—an antidote for a broken heart?' she added with a wry smile.

'I guess it is, Ellis,' he agreed after a moment. 'And it could be you're wise. Maybe I'm just selfish to want a daughter.'

'You're sweet,' she said, and put her hand over his.

No more was said on the subject after that. They had dinner, and at ten-thirty the cabaret show began. Ellis hadn't realised it was a nude show, and for the first few moments she felt more than a little shocked. All those beautiful girls with their fantastic headdresses and their bare breasts——

For some strange reason, she turned her head to see if the man in the velvet jacket was still there. He was, and he was looking not at the show but at her. Badly disconcerted, she turned swiftly away, and decided to put him completely out of her mind, and soon, because she began enjoying the show, she managed it. The sets and the lighting were lavish and dramatic and so were the costumes, and though it was the most sophisticated show she had ever seen in her life, it was not in the least vulgar, and the dancing and singing were really first class. Ellis supposed that with all that money coming in from the gaming tables, the management could well afford a production where no expense was spared!

When it was over and the lights went up, some of the performers—though not the nude ones!—came down to move about among the tables, and Jake told Ellis, 'I'll see if I can persuade a couple of the members of the cast to come and join us for a drink. Would you like that?'

She nodded smilingly. As a matter of fact, she would just as soon have called it a day and gone up to bed, but it would be unkind to reject Jake's efforts to amuse her. He really put himself out to do that, and she watched him go down the steps to speak to one of the male singers, then disappear somewhere at the side of the stage.

Ellis sat back in her chair to wait for him. Drink waiters were hovering, a few people were leaving their tables, probably to go into the casino which stayed open till three or four o'clock in the morning. It had been fun staying here, she reflected, and it had helped a little to take her mind off her unhappiness, but this sophisticated life wasn't really for her. The late nights had exhausted her a little, probably because she wasn't sleeping well. Once she was alone with her thoughts, they were all too likely to go to Paul, and she would remember his kisses, his caresses—the murmured words that after all had meant so little——

Unaware of it, she had been staring at a man who was coming towards her, and her nerves jumped and colour flooded her face as he stopped near her, his hand on the back of the chair that Jake had vacated.

'May I join you?' he asked her silkily, with a smile that bordered on a suggestive leer.

Ellis licked her top lip nervously. 'I'm—I'm waiting for someone.'

'Then let me buy you a drink while you're waiting,' he said, obviously not believing her. 'What would you like?'

'Nothing. I—I don't want a drink,' she stammered. He looked so determined she didn't know what to do, and helplessly she watched as he pulled out Jake's chair, then looked about for the drink waiter. Ellis repeated distinctly, though she was quailing inside, 'I don't want a drink, and that chair is—is reserved.'

Her words had absolutely no effect and she looked around her wildly for Jake but instead caught the eye of the man in the velvet jacket. He had risen from his chair and was coming purposefully towards the man who was pestering Ellis. She had no idea what it was he said to the other man, but it was certainly effective, for with a shrug, and without another word to Ellis, he took himself off.

Ellis looked up at her rescuer to thank him and found herself staring into eyes that were green and hard and mocking, and totally devoid of anything resembling sympathy, and she felt herself stiffen instinctively.

'Thank you,' she said indistinctly, discovering her throat to be suddenly dry, and added, reacting to his expression, 'You needn't really have bothered. I can—I can cope.'

He raised dark eyebrows that, unlike his hair, were untouched by silver. 'Well then, you can cope with me, now that we're alone,' he said dryly. 'We'll see how you make out.'

She parted her lips to protest, but without any regard for her wishes he pulled out Jake's chair and sat down opposite her, then turned and summoned the waiter.

'What are you drinking?' he asked her with a lift of his brow.

'Nothing,' she said icily, reflecting she had merely exchanged one unwelcome companion for another.

She saw his mouth quirk. He told the waiter, 'A Dubonnet for the lady with ice and orange juice, and a Scotch for me,' then returned his attention to Ellis, and, in particular, to the bracelet glittering at her wrist. Instinctively she removed her arm from the table where it had been resting and then wished she hadn't. It looked somehow guilty, and she raised her hand to touch her hair.

He said appreciatively, 'Real sapphires. Quite a nice little gift to receive before dinner—or even after it.'

She bristled at his obvious implication—but of course she had known what conclusions he had drawn about her and Jake before. She had told herself she didn't care then, but somehow it was different when someone was sitting face to face with you and as good as telling you he thought you were immoral. She tossed up between a casual, 'Yes—it is nice, isn't it?' and a strong desire to tell him to mind his own business, and the latter impulse won.

'I don't know quite what you're suggesting,' she said distantly, 'but I think you have a nasty mind, and I wish you'd mind your own business. I—I didn't invite you to join me.'

'I don't have a particularly nasty mind,' he said calmly, 'but I happen to be a realist. As for invitations —your eyes have been throwing them around very generously tonight. And a display of female charm is an invitation in itself at any time.' His greenish eyes moved from her face to the smoothness of her shoulders and the swelling curve of her breasts beneath the soft stuff of her gown. Then he leaned forward and looked intently into the blue of her eyes, his shoulders against the light broad and intimidating. 'Your boy-friend's too old for you,' he said flatly.

Ellis gasped and stifled a retort as the drink waiter set two glasses on the table, and though she had not meant to touch hers, she raised it to her lips and took a long swallow to cool herself down before she said frigidly, 'You're—you're insufferable! And for your information, Jake's not—he—he happens to be an old family friend.'

The senusual mouth curved mockingly as he picked up his Scotch.

'That sounds like a bedtime story to me. I've watched you together—his eyes were clambering all over you like a bee bumbling about in a flowercup full of honey ... What are you going to tell me next? That it's your twenty-first birthday and he's giving you a good time because you're a poor little orphan with no one to love you?'

Her cheeks flamed, more at the way he was looking at her than at what he actually said, and she stammered confusedly, 'I—I am an orphan, and he's giving me a good time because——' She stopped and swallowed. Next thing she'd be telling him about Paul and her broken love affair, and heaven knew what interpretation he'd put on a confession like that. She tried again and told a blatant lie, surprising even herself. 'As a matter of fact, this bracelet happens to be a—an engagement present.'

An unguarded flash of surprise lit the cynicism in his eyes, and he looked over his glass at her ringless left hand.

'An engagement present of such quality—but no engagement ring. Looks like somebody's slipped up.'

She had, he meant, of course, and she improvised swiftly, 'I don't have a ring yet because—because it's only just happened today—over the telephone. My

fiancé lives on—on Flinders Island. I'll be joining him
there in a day or two—I'll get my ring *then*.'

That, she thought with a small feeling of triumph,
appeared to have put him in his place, for he said nothing more until he'd finished his whisky. Then he commented thoughtfully, 'I wouldn't have imagined you
were Flinders Island material. Have you been there?'

'Not yet. But I've read something about it.'

'I wouldn't mind betting there's a shock in store for
you. It's hardly like the Casino Hotel, you know—it's
the other end of the earth, in fact.'

She shrugged indifferently. 'I happen to like quiet
places.'

His lips quirked. 'That's just a little too hard to believe. Well, here comes the old family friend, so I'll
leave you to his tender care.' He rose to his feet, bow-
ing slightly, and Ellis noticed for the first time how big
and powerfully built he was. Then before he sauntered
away, he told her mockingly, 'We'll meet again, without a doubt.'

'I hope *not*,' she breathed, but she didn't think he
heard her.

Jake had two members of the cabaret cast with him,
and he looked pleased with himself. He sent Ellis a
questioning look, motioning with a slight gesture of his
head towards the man who had been occupying his seat
and was now making his way to the exit.

Ellis murmured with a strained smile, 'It's all right,
Jake,' and then Jake introduced the two dancers,
Sherry and Michael, and there was a bit of business
about finding a larger table. Champagne was ordered,
and for the next hour or so Ellis did her best to be light-
hearted and gay and to make herself good company so
that Jake would be satisfied his treatment was effective.
At least that man was not there to stare at her and draw

his evil conclusions, she thought, and that in itself was a help.

'You've enjoyed yourself tonight, haven't you, darling?' Jake said with satisfaction after the little party of four had split up. Sherry and Michael had gone and she and Jake were in the casino, his arm lightly around her waist. 'What about trying your luck at one of the tables?'

Ellis shook her head. 'No, thanks, Jake. I'm ready for bed.' She stifled a yawn smilingly. 'I'm not used to all this social life, you know.'

'Well then, so long as you're not going to lie awake thinking of that fellow——'

'I won't,' she assured him. 'I'll be asleep the minute my head touches the pillow.' To her relief he accepted that, saw her to the elevator, and kissed her lightly before she stepped into it.

Later, in bed, she did lie awake—thinking of Paul as she always did, remembering his kisses, the excitement of being with him. For a while she fantasised about what might have happened if she had looked then as she did now—had owned all those pretty, glamorous clothes. They'd have been safely engaged before Jan came back—she wouldn't be here in Hobart in her present dilemma. She'd never have thought about working for a farmer on Flinders Island, never have written Steve Gascoyne that letter.

Her mind wandered back to the night she had decided to write and offer to come and work for him. Paul had come to dinner that night, but as Jan's guest, not hers. Ellis had cooked the meal, as she always did, the main course being a particular favourite of Paul's—curried prawns, which Ellis made with cream and green peppers and ginger, and all sorts of delicate flavourings. Afterwards, alone in the kitchen, she had washed up the dishes while her uncle, who had his office at home, did some work and Jan and Paul sat in the softly lit sitting room, listening to music.

Ellis knew better than to go and join them when she'd tidied the kitchen. Instead, she went out for a long walk, feeling very lonely and heartsick, and wishing she could run away. When she came back, Paul's car was still there, and she went straight upstairs to bed. But she found it impossible to sleep and at somewhere around two o'clock she had got out of bed and gone restlessly to the window. She saw Paul's car in the drive, and the soft rose glow of light falling through Jan's bedroom curtains, and she drew back, somehow shocked and full of despair. She had gone back to bed to lie rigid and sleepless. Paul had never come to her room—never ever suggested he should. And she wouldn't have allowed it—much as she loved him. Oh, never in a million years! She was too unsophisticated for him, she had thought bitterly. Now he had forgotten her—he thought only of Jan.

Ellis had felt as if her heart would break.

Then, gradually, her thoughts had moved from herself and her wretchedness to Steve Gascoyne, the man whom Jan had jilted so heartlessly. Was he now feeling as bereft and lonely and unhappy as she was, alone on his sheep station?

Some mad impulse added to the sheer inability to sleep made her leave her bed again, switch on the reading light, and sit down and write him a letter. It had come to her almost without conscious thought that they could help each other, she and this farmer. She could never make up to him for the loss of Jan, just as he could never make up to her for the loss of Paul, but as they were both in the same situation they could help each other. She was desperate to get away from her uncle's house and the torture of seeing Jan and Paul together. A week with Jake would not be enough, she knew she couldn't come back here. And he—he would surely be only too grateful to have someone to look after his house, to cook for his shearers and so on, from what Jan had said.

Ellis didn't remember afterwards exactly what she had written in a rather long and rambling letter, but the gist of it was their reciprocal need of each other. She told him she would be in Hobart and asked him please to write to her at the Casino Hotel, and promised she would fly to Finders Island the very moment she heard from him.

Disappointingly, and incomprehensibly, she hadn't heard from him. But perhaps tomorrow——

Ellis turned on her side and determinedly closed her eyes. She simply must get some sleep! But, annoyingly, into her mind drifted an image of that man in the cabaret room with his green eyes, his tanned face, his horrible mind. She certainly didn't want to think about *him*, and she banished his face determinedly. He was one person she never wanted to see again—and if she were unlucky enough to come within sight of him in the hotel tomorrow, she would turn her back and walk the other way. She was quite determined they *wouldn't* meet again, despite his parting words.

Somehow or other Ellis fell asleep at last, but she woke late the following morning. Jake always breakfasted in his room and rose very late, seeing he stayed up till all hours of the night, and he was not around when at last she went down to breakfast in the Coffee Shoppe. She chose a table by the big windows that looked out on Sandy Bay, and as she ate she tried not to worry about what she was going to do with her future.

Breakfast over, she went hopefully to the foyer to see if there was a letter for her from Steve Gascoyne.

Nothing again. She bit her lip in vexation. Surely she'd have heard by now if he were interested. She was beginning to think that in his bitterness he might have torn her letter up when he discovered she was a cousin of Jan Webster's. She had felt so sincerely that she could help him—but perhaps he'd already found a housekeeper. In which case, it would have been polite of him to let her know.

Jake came down to the foyer a few minutes later, and they spent the rest of the day together in Hobart.

'Do you realise this is the last day of our holiday together?' Jake asked her. 'And since you haven't heard from your farmer, how about thinking again of coming back to Adelaide with me? I'm going to miss you, you know, Ellis.'

It was certainly tempting while she was feeling so deflated, so lost, but it would be the easy way out and life, Ellis thought, was not meant to be easy. Not if it was to be worth while. She knew there was more satisfaction to be had out of struggling for happiness than out of taking the line of least resistance, the easy way that didn't lead to a really personal goal. Besides, there was Pat. So she told Jake affectionately, 'I'll miss you too. But I'm a working girl at heart, Jake darling, and I'll find something to do. If I don't, I promise I'll come to you.'

After they'd lunched at the Ferntree Tavern, Jake was all set to go on another shopping spree, but Ellis firmly refused and suggested instead that they should take a car and drive to the top of Mount Wellington, so often shrouded in cloud or mist but today standing out indomitably against a clear blue sunny sky. She rather suspected that it wasn't quite Jake's cup of tea, that he enjoyed the bustle of the city, but for her there was immense pleasure in looking down from the top of the towering mountain on to Australia's second oldest city—small but beautiful—spread out on the two shores of the Derwent River.

She felt considerably more cheerful somehow when they returned to the hotel towards evening.

In her room in the tower block, she showered and reflected with satisfaction that she had got through the day without encountering that—that green-eyed monster again. Now there was only tonight left—and dear heaven, she was going to have to come up with some sort of story about what she planned to do when Jake left in the morning. Otherwise he would probably refuse to leave her here.

Emerging from the shower, she towelled herself dry and slipped into a pale blue dressing gown. She reached for the *Mercury*, that was delivered to the room each morning, and sitting down she ran her eye anxiously over the positions vacant column. 'Live in on farm— help with housework and children—motherly woman,' she read. There was nothing, really, and the mad idea entered her head that she might see if there was anything available at the hotel—perhaps in one of the shops on the mezzanine floor. Not that she fancied that sort of a job, but——

Someone knocked on her door, and when she opened it Jake was there. They were dining in the revolving restaurant tonight and he looked very handsome in his dark suit, white shirt and plain wine-coloured tie.

'May I come in, Ellis? I'm getting worried about you with nothing arranged and I don't want to spoil your dinner discussing it. The fact is, I simply must go to-morrow—I've promised Pat I'll be there for some special dinner we've been invited to.' He came into the room as he spoke, but instead of taking one of the chairs prowled restlessly around. 'Something's got to be settled about you tonight. I refuse to leave you here in a void ... Can't I persuade you to come back with me after all?'

Ellis shook her head. 'No—really, Jake. I'm just positive I'll hear from Mr Gascoyne tomorrow,' she lied.

He stopped pacing and eyed her ruefully. 'Ellis, be practical! Suppose you don't hear—and you're here all alone—Oh, I'd pay for you to stay as long as you wanted to, but you're so young! I realise it anew now I'm seeing you without your make-up. And as a matter of fact, I'm far from happy even when I think about you working for this farmer. Someone ought to check up and make sure you're not stepping into something—shady.'

Ellis gave a little laugh. 'On Flinders Island? I'm told it's the end of the earth! It's probably the safest place in the world I could go to. Besides, Martin's still there.'

'Well, that's something,' Jake conceded, and at that moment the telephone rang.

Jake, who happened to be near it, automatically reached out and lifted the receiver. 'Hello?' He gave the room number, and then—'Yes, Miss Lincoln's right here. Hang on a moment.' He held out the receiver. 'For you, Ellis.'

'Hello?' Ellis wondered who on earth could be telephoning her, and then her heart gave a leap as the voice at the other end of the line said, 'Steve Gascoyne, Miss Lincoln. About that letter you wrote me——'

'Oh yes!' Ellis exclaimed eagerly. She had known it would happen! 'Are you—are you interested, Mr Gascoyne? I've been waiting to hear from you.'

'I've been away from home, and your letter's only just reached me. I'm in Hobart, right here at the hotel as a matter of fact, so we can meet.'

'You—you want me to come?' she insisted. 'I'm quite free—I can come tomorrow——'

'Don't rush it, Miss Lincoln,' he interrupted. Through her nervousness and excitement she thought vaguely that it was a curiously familiar voice, but she didn't realise why until later. 'I want to see you before rash decisions are made on either of our parts ... Can you have dinner with me?'

Ellis glanced across at Jake, who was listening openly. She wondered fleetingly if she should ask Mr Gascoyne to join them, but decided not. She didn't want Jake in on this—she wanted, rather obstinately, to make her own decision.

'Well?' The voice sounded rather impatient.

'No, I can't,' she said quickly. 'I've made other arrangements.'

'You've what?' he asked in a curiously thoughtful tone that gave her the impression he had heard what she said and merely wanted to have her say it again.

'I have a dinner date,' she said.

'Oh, I see. Well, I'm leaving tomorrow, so if you'll come to my suite right away we'll have a few minutes to look each other over. I'll expect you shortly.' He gave her his room number and hung up, and Ellis, feeling slightly dazed and unsure whether he seemed interested or not, told Jake unnecessarily and rather breathlessly, 'That was Mr Gascoyne. He's here, and he wants to see me about that position—now. I'll—I'll have to get dressed.'

Jake nodded. 'Shall I come along with you, Ellis?

I'm a more experienced judge of character than you are, and I'd like to know what you're letting yourself in for.'

'No, really, it will be quite all right,' she said quickly. 'If I have any doubts I won't commit myself.'

'That's sensible,' Jake approved. 'You don't have to accept the first thing that comes along ... Well, I'd better let you dress. I'll be downstairs in the Birdcage Bar. Join me there when your interview's over—and it might be a good idea to bring this fellow along so I can meet him. Our table's booked for nine o'clock, so we've plenty of time. Right?'

'Right,' Ellis agreed, and when he had gone she stood motionless for a moment. Something was bothering her at the back of her mind, but she felt too flustered to dig it out, and switching her attention to what she should wear, she went to the wardrobe. Reason told her she had better wear something neat and sensible, because her age, that she hadn't mentioned in her letter, was somewhat against her when it came to taking on the responsibility of someone else's house.

A frown creased her brow. The wardrobe was filled with the pretty, expensive clothes Jake had lavished on her. There was nothing there in the least sober and sedate-looking. She turned away and rummaged in her suitcase, and rooted out a long-sleeved white blouse and a slim black skirt. That was more like it. Only before she joined Jake she would have to change. She didn't really think, in any case, that she'd ask Mr Gascoyne down to the Birdcage Bar to meet Jake. There would be a little awkwardness about introducing him, about explaining how she came to be spending a holiday with him. It would be different if he were her uncle, but as it was he was too good-looking and gallant, and she didn't want to go into detailed explanations.

So, she told herself with a shrug, she had better depend on her own judgment entirely. Anyhow, what was she worrying about? That poor sheep farmer from a tiny island! He was sure to be absolutely dependable, and she felt more certain than ever that Jan had merely been amusing herself with him to entertain herself during her holiday.

Except—his voice over the phone hadn't sounded slow and drawling and countryfied. Not even frightfully Australian. Well, a sheep farmer could be well educated, couldn't he? she reminded herself.

She tossed off her gown and in seconds had stepped into the skirt and buttoned up her blouse to its rather demure neck. She looked at herself critically in the mirror. She did look young without her make-up, as Jake had said, but though it might add sophistication, she decided not to use it. She'd stress the practical side of her personality. She rather wished now she hadn't had her hair cut. Drawn back from her face and caught in a neat knob at her nape, it had given her a certain staid quality. Now her golden-brown locks had been styled so expertly and cunningly that her hair stood out and framed her pale face in a sophisticatedly sculptured fashion that completely changed her personality. It was impossible to make herself look like the Ellis Lincoln who had kept house so assiduously for Uncle Bill.

Hastily she dragged a filmy black scarf from the drawer and tied it loosely around her head, confining her gleaming hair. She looked at herself critically. Now she looked more circumspect! And, in fact, without lipstick or eyeshadow, she looked encouragingly prim and proper.

So she thought, unaware that the blue dazzle of her

eyes when she raised her dark lashes destroyed that effect utterly.

Not many moments later she was stepping out of the elevator and walking along the thickly carpeted hallway to Steven Gascoyne's suite. Her heart was beating fast. She had been waiting for this to happen. She had assured Jake it was what she really wanted. Yet now, unaccountably, she was aware that some part of her was drawing back. She even began to wonder if she had been a fool to write that impulsive letter to the unknown man her cousin had jilted so callously. After all, she really hadn't the least idea what he was like. Her mental picture of him was purely imaginary. She wondered too if she had indiscreetly bared some part of her soul in what she had written in those sleepless hours of the early morning.

Her footsteps had slowed, but now with a slight shock she realised she was standing outside the door of his suite. She very nearly turned on her heel and went silently away, mad images floating through her mind of herself telling Jake she had decided against the job after all. That would mean she'd have to go to Adelaide, and once she was there, would Jake use his wiles to persuade her to continue the idle life? And how would she get on with Pat? After all, the marriage hadn't taken place yet. Pat might decide it wasn't for her if there was an—unofficial stepdaughter around.

Ellis braced herself, and with a feeling that fate was pushing her on, she raised her hand and knocked, and in the very instant that she did so she realised in a flash what was at the back of her reluctance—why she was feeling so churned up.

That voice on the telephone! Of course—it had reminded her of the voice of the—the green-eyed monster! Yet it couldn't be his. No way in the world could she persuade herself that *that* man was her nice sheep farmer. The very thought was ludicrous.

But when a second later the door was opened to her, her fears were realised. It was the man with the cynical green eyes.

CHAPTER TWO

QUITE obviously he was nothing like as surprised—or shocked—as she was, and his hard green gaze moved deliberately over her, from the black scarf confining her hair to the tips of her high-heeled black sandals. By the time it returned to her face, so innocently devoid of make-up, the rose colour that had come into her cheeks had subsided, leaving them pale.

She licked her lips and swallowed on a dry throat.

'Are you—are you Mr Gascoyne?' she asked, and crazily she willed him to say no, that she'd come to the wrong suite, or that Mr Gascoyne was waiting for her inside.

'That's right,' he agreed, reaching out to take hold of her arm and draw her into the room. 'And you, of course, are Ellis Lincoln. I thought I recognised your voice over the telephone, though I doubted my ears. You're hardly the heartbroken little creature I'd been expecting from the tone of your letter, but then you've been consoling yourself already, haven't you?'

Ellis slid away from his hands. All the thoughts she had harboured of somehow making amends for Jan's behaviour now seemed quite absurd. She couldn't even imagine this man needing help, let alone having a broken heart. He was nothing like the man she had envisaged herself working for—the simple countryman her cousin had treated so cruelly—and she was already well aware of his opinion of her.

'Look, Mr Gascoyne,' she said, trying to keep her voice calm and even, 'we needn't go on with this, need we? I—I know you're not interested——'

'Then you know wrong. I'm very interested,' he said smoothly. The door clicked shut, and helplessly, Ellis took a few more steps into the room, then sank into the armchair he indicated mainly because suddenly her legs felt in danger of giving way. She had just remembered she'd told him she was engaged to a man on Flinders Island. *That* was going to take some explaining, and all she really wanted was to get out of here quickly. She kept her lashes lowered defensively, acutely aware that he was once more scrutinising her.

'You're quite a new proposition this evening, aren't you?' he pronounced after what seemed an endless time. 'Now you've scrubbed off your make-up and got into some—lamb's clothing. It's lucky we'd already met last night.'

'Lucky?' she repeated, her hand going nervously to the neck of her neat white blouse.

'Yes. For both of us.' He took a chair facing her and stretched out long legs, muscular-looking in well-cut dark pants. 'Do you know what you remind me of at this instant?'

He sounded amused, and though it was a purely rhetorical question she shook her head, and as if compelled glanced up to meet his eyes, then recoiled inwardly from their cynicism and worldliness.

'You're like a little moonbird chick,' he said ruminatively. 'Sitting warm and well fed in its burrow happily unaware that at any tick of the clock someone will come along and scoop it up for dinner.' His wide mouth curved faintly in a mocking smile. 'But you're no innocent chick, are you, Ellis, so I'm not impressed. And it's good luck for you I haven't been fooled, or I might say no to your prettily put suggestion you should come over to Flinders to live with me.'

Ellis stared at him, her mouth falling slightly open, her eyes wide. What on earth was he talking about? She asked the question aloud, and he ran impatient fingers through the thick black and silver of his hair.

'My dear girl, your appearance would have thrown me. If I hadn't seen you living it up with your ageing Romeo, I'd have believed in you as the broken reed you made yourself out to be when you wrote to me. And my taste doesn't run to—innocents.'

'To—to innocents?' Ellis repeated foolishly. 'What's that to do with—with keeping house, and—and cooking for the shearers?'

'Not a thing,' he said laconically. He raised one dark eyebrow and his eyes skimmed over her. 'But I'm hardly picturing you in that role. I'm envisaging you in my bed.'

Ellis stifled a gasp and the colour rushed to her face. 'I—I don't know what you mean,' she said huskily.

'Of course you know what I mean. Your cousin was going to marry me and you offered to take her place.'

'I didn't offer to take Jan's place!' she exclaimed hotly. 'I offered to—to do your housekeeping and cook for the shearers.'

He looked slightly amused. 'Those shearers are really on your mind, aren't they? Well, that's great—but you had other things on your mind when you wrote to me that decidedly come-on letter I received this evening when I came back to the hotel.' He screwed up his eyes and leaned back in his chair. 'It was half past three in the morning, you said. You'd been lying sleepless in bed thinking of me and of how you and I should get together. Our hearts were broken, our lives were shattered—we *needed* each other. Jan had taken your man, why shouldn't you and I team up—do a swap, as it were.'

Ellis's pulses were racing. She hadn't written those things! But had she implied them? Crazily, she didn't know. It was all too possible—she *had* thought they needed each other; he needed a housekeeper, she needed a job. That was what she had meant, and she told him determinedly, even though her voice shook slightly, 'I meant we could team up in a—a certain way. I thought you needed a housekeeper, and as I needed a job, it was an opportunity. Or—or has your aunt come back? Jan said she'd been taken to hospital——'

His dark face grew sombre and his lips tightened. 'No, my aunt hasn't come back. I attended her funeral two days ago, and I've been seeing to her affairs today.'

She caught her lower lip between her teeth. 'I'm sorry.'

There was a moment of silence which she at least found awkward, then she said practically, deciding to forget the things he had said that had shocked her, 'I can be of use to you, then, Mr Gascoyne. I'm a responsible person, I assure you. I've kept house for my uncle for several years.' She stopped. The way he was looking at her she was mad to be trying to persuade him. He wasn't at all the kind of man she wanted to work for.

He reached into the pocket of the dark coat he wore and produced cigarettes. He offered her one and when she declined it lit one for himself, doing it slowly, a thoughtful look on his hard, handsome face.

'Well then, I'm offering you a job,' he said at last. 'But it's a double-sided proposition. I can do with a woman in the kitchen, but more than anything I need a woman in my bed, not merely to satisfy my sexual appetite but to give me sons. It's not all that easy for a man living the life I do on a sparsely populated island to find himself a wife. I'm thirty-six and aware of a growing urgency. Jan would have done admirably, but as things are, I'm quite willing to settle for you,' he finished, and his eyes looked straight into hers.

She felt a shock go through her and she drew a deep breath. This just couldn't be happening! She asked unevenly, 'Couldn't you—couldn't you find someone in Hobart while you're here?'

'I have,' he said unequivocally. 'You.' Through half-closed eyes that glittered green and oddly menacing in the artificial light, he regarded her intently. 'You gave yourself away last night, you know,' he said with soft irony. 'Aren't I the man on Flinders Island you're engaged to?'

She swallowed nervously. 'Of course not! I—I made that up. I didn't like the sort of thing you were thinking about me.'

'You mean you didn't like my hardly surprising scepticism about the old family friend?'

'Yes. Because Jake's not—he only wants to——'

He broke in abruptly. 'Don't tell me what he wants. I can guess. And my guess is more likely to approximate to the truth than anything you'll tell me. My experience of the female sex has taught me that cheating and double-dealing are as essential a part of a woman's make-up as seeds are part of the passion-fruit.'

'I'm not a cheat!' she exclaimed, infuriated.

'No? Then why the disguise tonight? Why the black scarf—the office-girl blouse buttoned so chastely over your charms? Of course you're a cheat.'

Ellis's blue eyes were angry, and through her anger she was aware that she had tried to make herself look —different. She got to her feet and said coldly, 'If you think that of me then there's no point in our going on with this discussion, is there? You don't want me on your sheep farm.'

'Of course I want you on Warrianda,' he contradicted. He had risen too and stood, hands on his narrow hips, confronting her. 'You can take over, in fact, right where your cousin left off, and just as soon as you like.'

She looked at him suspiciously. 'What's that supposed to mean?'

His smile was cynical. 'You know Jan, you should be able to guess. But don't forget, I'm offering to make an honest woman of you.'

'You—you must be fooling,' she said after a moment. 'You can't just decide like that to—to marry someone you don't even know. Not when you've been—not when your heart's been broken,' she finished uncertainly.

He smiled, but his eyes were hard, 'Not when I've been jilted?' he said, and his voice was equally hard. 'Let's not be afraid to say it. As for my heart, it's unbreakable. It's as hard as iron. My guess is you're thinking in terms of yourself. You've been jilted too, haven't you? You think your tender little heart's been broken. Are you by any chance cherishing a hope that your boy-friend will tire of Jan and want you back after all?'

'No,' she said stiffly, ignoring the pain his words caused her. 'I don't think that will happen. Jan's very attractive to men. She always has been. I'm the plain one,' she finished bitterly.

'That's a lot of eyewash and you know it,' he said dismissively. 'Plain girls don't get sapphire bracelets given them to celebrate non-existent engagements— not even by old family friends. They don't even get offers of marriage from strangers as a rule. In fact, if you were plain—a little nondescript—a frump— *I* wouldn't be interested in you. Unattractive looks are the result of an unattractive character, in my opinion ... So now we're back to the purpose of this encounter. We've met, I've made my decision, and the job's yours if you want it. Do you want it?'

Ellis bit her lip. She felt totally confused, and she didn't even know what he was offering her. She wanted a job, but she certainly didn't want to marry this man, and she hated him for thinking she was the sort of girl who'd even contemplate it. She couldn't understand why he should be so willing to put *her* in Jan's place, either. What *did* he feel about Jan? He said his heart wasn't broken, but it would be pride that made him say that, and in fact, he might merely be intent on showing Jan how little he cared that she had left him.

She said helplessly, 'I need a job. I—I don't want to go back to live with my uncle and Jan. And—and I couldn't possibly live with Jake——'

'The old family friend,' he put in dryly. 'I told you last night he's too old for you, so I applaud *that* decision, if this is a sample of the kind of life he leads—you'd grow fat and lazy and uninteresting in no time at all if you settled down as his mistress.'

Ellis said on a breath, 'You're so insufferably insulting, Mr Gascoyne, I really don't know why I don't just walk out on you. I'm not any man's mistress and I don't want to be, and this is the—the craziest interview I've ever been involved in. I wish now I'd let Jake come with me to your suite—then you wouldn't have dared say half the things you have.'

He looked at her thoughtfully, his green eyes narrowed. 'Jake answered your phone, didn't he?'

She coloured hotly. 'Yes, but that doesn't mean——'

'Don't bother explaining what it doesn't mean,' he interrupted crisply. 'I don't claim the right to ask questions. As for the things I've said to you, this interview has been a surprise to me too, you know. I didn't think

I'd be in for anything one half so involved, when all I need, quite simply, is a woman.'

He broke off and she felt the silence, and she felt his eyes scorching her.

'I—don't need a—man,' she said indistinctly.

'Every woman does,' he said, and without warning he reached for her. In a second, her body was clamped against his with a closeness that shocked her. Holding her captive with an arm that was iron-hard, he used his free hand to pull the scarf from her head, and she saw it snake to the floor even as she felt the power of his long fingers raking through the uncovered silk of her hair.

'You're too much like a nun in that black thing,' he muttered. 'I can't touch you when you look like that.'

And then he was kissing her as Paul had never kissed her. Some part of her consciousness detached itself briefly to become involved with Paul and his pleasurable, temperate kisses, but such intense and sensual responses were clamouring for possession of her body that she was soon lost, and all control over her own mind vanished. Their bodies were so closely locked together she was inevitably conscious of the fact that his passion was aroused—in what she knew must be a purely animal way because certainly there was no tenderness between them. The intimacy of the contact was becoming unbearable to her, and she struggled futilely against his strength as his hand found its way inside her blouse to her breast. Despite herself, she quickened to his experienced touch, and sensations that were entirely new to her pulsed through her nerves excitingly.

For a long moment everything in the world seemed to fade into nothingness except her own sexuality, and then with a supreme effort she wrenched herself violently away from him.

She stood quivering, her eyes closed, swallowing on some emotion that rose in her throat. She felt bruised, violated, and she couldn't look at him. Dimly she wished she could run from the room, forget this man, obliterate him from her life. Go back to an innocence that, insanely, now seemed far away and unattainable.

They were incoherent, fragmentary thoughts, and she didn't move, but stayed helplessly where she was, her head bowed.

She still didn't move when a muscular arm came round her shoulders to steady her, and a male voice, warm against her loosened hair, said softly, 'So you're a virgin, are you? I wouldn't have believed it—not after watching you in action last night.'

Ellis didn't answer. She hadn't got control of herself yet, and she stood passively, not even pushing away that arm that lay lightly across her shoulders.

'I'd better let you go,' he said after a moment. 'Go down to your room and give your face a good splashing with cold water. You'll soon feel able to face up to your dinner date.'

Ellis started, thinking of Jake. With a feeling of inner panic she let Steve Gascoyne take her to the elevator— see her into it. It was empty, and the door slid shut, locking him out. Somehow or other she got back to her room, and there she shut the door and stood in the silence and emptiness with only her own reflection to witness the emotions that passed across her face.

Her job on Flinders Island had vanished. It was something she'd never think of again, once she'd told Jake.

'So that's that.' She said the matter-of-fact words aloud as she stared vacantly across at the mirror, at the white blur of her face, the dark gold cloud of her hair. Then with an effort, she moved. Jake would think she was never coming if she didn't hurry.

With fingers that were unaccustomedly clumsy, she unbuttoned her blouse—though some of the buttons were already undone—then stepped out of her skirt and, going into the bathroom that opened off her room, splashed and splashed her face with cold water.

He had said that if she did that she'd soon feel able to face up to her dinner date, and it was funny, but it did help. Her cheeks were pink now, and the blue eyes that looked back at her from the mirror over the wash-basin were bright, and a rather pale and wavering smile curved her lips. So she was alive after all, and nothing dreadful had happened to her, had it? She hadn't been raped, she had merely been brought to some sort of discovery about her sexual self—a discovery that somehow shocked her, and that she refused to think about just now.

Back in the bedroom, she pulled a long-skirted dress from the wardrobe and slipped into it. It was a floating thing of blue and violet silk with a soft round neckline, and long full sleeves caught in at the wrist. She knew it suited her colouring and she loved the feel of it and she began to feel fully recovered. She used mascara and eye-shadow and brushed out her hair, then on her way to the door she stood stock still. What was she going to do? Look in the *Mercury* again tomorrow? But Jake wouldn't leave her here. Oh, why couldn't that hateful man have turned out to be the pleasant farmer she had imagined? Then there'd have been no crazy interview—no humiliating climax to it. What kind of a man was he, for goodness' sake? And what sort of an affair had he had with Jan? She'd thought Jan was the cruel one, but he'd said his heart was hard as iron. Hadn't he even been in love with Jan? Had he simply needed a wife and decided that she would do? And then Jan had broken it off. She didn't want a double-sided marriage any more than Ellis wanted a double-sided job. He was so hard, so cynical, she was almost convinced he had been as cold-blooded in his attitude towards her cousin as he was towards her.

Almost, but not quite. Because Jan was so lovely, so vivacious, she must have stirred something in him. Ellis didn't know how many men had fallen in love with Jan. They fell for her with no effort at all.

Her thoughts screeched to a halt. *Paul* had fallen in love with Jan with no effort at all.

She felt the old blackness engulf her mind as the pain of losing Paul came back. Once again she was reaching out helplessly in the dark, turning every way to find some means of escape, of forgetfulness. The pain of ended love was like that. You thought it had eased, you thought you'd found some way not to re-member it, and then—a stray thought—and it was all back, as shatteringly destructive as ever, and the pitiful little bit of confidence you'd regained disappeared like a star behind the secretly gathered clouds of night.

Ellis looked down at her lovely gown, at the evening purse that glittered in her hand and felt herself abso-lutely nothing. She felt herself shrivel away to complete and utter insignificance—because Paul didn't love her.

But that man—that outrageous, insufferably rude man Steve Gascoyne—he had intimated so casually that he would make her his wife. And he had taught her in a few minutes something that Paul had never taught her—the reality of her own sexual nature. Suddenly she bit her lip so hard she tasted blood, and as she groped for a tissue and dabbed at it, someone knocked at her door. Jake—to see why she hadn't come down to the Birdcage Bar.

But it wasn't Jake, it was Steve Gascoyne, immaculate

in dark dinner suit and white shirt, her scarf in his hands. She felt a shiver run through the length of her body as their eyes met, and she almost snatched the scarf from him.

'You needn't have bothered about that,' she said ungraciously.

'I realise that. It was merely an excuse—if an excuse should be needed.' He looked over her shoulder into the room. 'You're alone?'

'Yes, of course,' she said sharply.

'May I come in for a moment?'

Her lashes flicked up in alarm, but before she could answer he was in the room and the door was shut and his back was against it.

'Jake's waiting for me,' she said edgily. She was unnerved by the way he looked at her. Somehow, instead of being conscious that she was no longer in her lamb's clothing, as he had put it, she could think only of the stroking touch of his fingers burning on her naked breast, rousing her—— She felt her breathing quicken, and barely managed to ask him, 'What do you want? To—to apologise?'

'I'm not a great believer in apologies. But we hadn't finshed our discussion. Now you've composed yourself, I've a different proposition to put to you. You can have that job if you want it——'

'You told me that before,' she said swiftly. 'But no, thank you—I'm not interested in—in double-sided jobs.'

'Oh, forget about that,' he said. 'I mean you can have it your way. You can housekeep for me—cook for the shearers. Come to Warrianda, anyhow, and we'll see how you can handle it. For all I know, you might be quite useless.'

'I'm not,' she retorted. 'I'm a good housekeeper.'

'Trustworthy too?' he said mockingly.

'Don't worry, I won't cheat you over your accounts.'

'You'll come, then? You're seriously interested?'

She licked her top lip nervously. Hadn't she told herself she didn't want to see this green-eyed monster again? Didn't she want to forget everything about him? And wouldn't it be crazy, knowing what she did about him, voluntarily to work under his roof? Yet if it was as *she* wanted it, if she was to be no more than his housekeeper—then why not? At least it was a way out of her dilemma. Almost as she reasoned with herself, she was telling him, 'Yes, of course I'm seriously interested. In the work,' she added.

'Of course,' he said without the trace of a smile. 'Then be ready to leave tomorrow after lunch, will you? I have one or two things to deal with in the morning, so it will be safest to make it then.'

Ellis nodded, and without saying any more he went. She drew a deep breath. She didn't know what she'd done or why she'd done it, and she knew she'd never acted with such reckless lack of logic in all her life.

She switched off the light and went down to the Birdcage Bar.

It was funny, she reflected later, how easy it was to tell Jake she'd got a job on Flinders Island. She told it as though it was all so normal and ordinary, yet if Jake had known what had really gone on in Steve Gascoyne's suite, he'd have been ropeable.

'What kind of a fellow is he?' Jake asked.

She'd told him, lying as though it were second nature to her, that Mr Gascoyne had declined to join them for a drink and sent his apologies. 'He's not feeling terribly sociable. His aunt—the one who used to housekeep for him—has just died.'

Thank heaven they didn't see Steve. In the Birdcage

Bar, Ellis had a brandy and lime with the feeling she really needed it. Then they left the Bar with its long glittering silver and glass rods and its exotic murals of naked females to take the elevator up to the top of the tower and the plush splendour of the revolving restaurant. There, with the night-time panorama of Hobart Town spinning slowly around them—the shadow of Mount Wellington, the lights of the city, the glimmering water of Sandy Bay and the delicate curve of light that was the new Tasman Bridge—Ellis told Jake falsely that yes, she liked Mr Gascoyne, he was a very pleasant man, and he was very grateful to have someone to take over the household tasks and the feeding of the shearers.

'I'll be able to see Martin too,' she added with a lightheartedness that even in her own ears rang true, and she sipped white wine and ate her lobster Thermidor and was glad of the soft lights. She was amazed at how calm and reassuring she sounded and a little ashamed at the trusting way Jake believed every word she said as she whitewashed the character of the man she knew in her heart she should not be trusting—and in fact didn't.

'Well, I guess I can leave you with an easy mind, Ellis love,' said Jake. 'You've got what you wanted, but I'll admit I'm disappointed to be losing you. I know you and Pat would hit it off, and I've been enjoying the experience of having a beautiful young daughter. It could go on for ever as far as I'm concerned,' he added, smiling at her across the table. 'But at least I've helped you over the worst of your heartache, haven't I? You're quite chirpy tonight—and you're looking wonderful. I hope I'm to meet this sheep farmer before I leave, by the way.'

'Oh, I think so,' she lied. 'In the morning before you

go. He—he'd like to meet you too.' She had a strong idea that Jake wouldn't want to trust her to a man like Steve Gascoyne. He would be a lot happier if he retained the image of the kind-hearted, slightly harassed countryman she had tried to get across, and she trembled inwardly at the thought of what she was about to do. There was just no way she could convince herself she was being sensible. She wasn't. She just had to have a job, that was all. She was more or less being pushed into it by circumstances.

In the morning, for once, she and Jake breakfasted together in the Coffee Shoppe, and she told him without batting an eyelid that Mr Gascoyne had had to go out early to complete some business. Later, as she saw to his packing while he settled their account downstairs, she reflected somewhat uncomfortably on her behaviour. Steve Gascoyne, she knew, would not be in the least surprised by it. He'd see it merely as a form of the cheating and double-dealing he expected from the female sex.

Ellis went out to the taxi to see Jake off, and before they parted he insisted on giving her a very handsome sum of money, and remarked he was disappointed not to meet her farmer after all.

'Yes, it's a shame—you'd like him,' said Ellis, and blushed inwardly to hear herself. What on earth was happening to her? She supposed it was simply that she knew she was doing something foolish, yet she had had no alternative, and she could regard it more or less as a stopgap until she found something more suitable. But away at the back of her mind she knew that something had happened to her when Steve Gascoyne had kissed her the way he had. She had felt so humiliated and ashamed, and yet——

She stared out at the glittering waters of the Bay and

the boats rocking there. No, she told herself severely, she couldn't possibly want to experience that again. And anyway, it wouldn't happen. Steve Gascoyne had given in. He had seen it her way. She was to be his housekeeper and nothing more. He was going to have to find another woman to take into his bed and he knew it. She had left him in no doubt whatsoever about that.

CHAPTER THREE

NOT so many hourse later she discovered how wrong she was, as she sat beside Steve Gascoyne in his own small plane, looking down on the last of Tasmania before they flew over Banks Strait.

It had been a surprise to her when, having arranged to meet her in the foyer at a certain hour after lunch, he had broken the news to her that they would be flying to Flinders straight from Hobart, and that he would be the pilot. He was dressed casually in a dark red silk shirt and pale beige trousers, and she was bound to admit to herself that he looked impressive. She hadn't seen him in daylight before, and he had a decidedly rugged look with the thick black and silver of his hair slightly ruffled and his green eyes crinkled against the sun. His tan, away from the artificial lights of the hotel, no longer looked theatrically unreal, but was a clear indication that he spent a great deal of his time in the open. In fact, it began to seem possible to Ellis that he was, after all, a farmer instead of a sophisticated man about town.

She had chosen to wear the simplest of dresses in soft ivory-coloured cotton, with a violet scarf at the neck. Her legs were bare and she wore sandals that were casual rather than dressy. She hoped she had struck a happy medium and that he wouldn't make any sneering remarks about lamb's clothing.

During the first part of the flight she tried to imagine what it would be like at Warrianda, and she felt a nervous trembling inside her. Who, she wondered for the first time—and was amazed at her stupidity in not thinking of this before—would be there, in the house, apart from herself and Steve Gascoyne? Jan's letters home had been all about herself and Steve with the odd bit of news about Martin, and Ellis racked her brains in vain trying to recall people she had mentioned. Whitemark, she knew, was the main town, and Martin spent some of his time at the Interstate Hotel there, but really she was abysmally—and a little disturbingly —ignorant about the set-up at Warrianda.

Well, it was too late for regrets now. The patchwork paddocks and the wooded mountains of Tasmania were receding, there was the long froth of a white beach and then the lovely pale green waters of Banks Strait were down below. The plane seemed to hover, smooth and steady, and the engine hummed. Ellis had never been in such a small plane before and the day was so smooth and sunny it was incredible. She glanced at the man beside her, but he seemed totally withdrawn and unaware of her, and on his face was a brooding look that made her feel strangely cut off from him. He was an absolute stranger, and, disturbed, she looked away from him and down below where there were now tiny islands scattered on the blue-green water, bare and wild-looking with rocky shores, some of them no more than great jagged rocks, all but washed over by the sea.

She had just about brought herself to the point of breaking through that moody silence of Steve Gascoyne's to ask him brightly to tell her something about Warrianda, when his green eyes flicked to her face and he said, 'Those are the first small islands of the Furneaux Group. If you know your Australian history, you'll remember that they were discovered by Tobias Furneaux in 1773, when his ship was separated from Captain Cook's *Endeavour* by a storm. Down there—do

you see the island with the beach shaped like a cres-
cent moon?—and the silver roof among the trees?
That's my island.'

'Your island?' She looked at him in faint alarm. 'But
we're not——'

'No, we're not going there now, I'm not doing that
to you,' he said, and sent her a dark look. 'I run cattle
there, and of necessity I make periodic visits. I named
it Disillusion Island, and I spent two years of my life
there.'

There was something brooding in his tone that made
her catch her breath, and the exclamation that it was
not a happy name was stifled even as it sprang to her
lips. Why had he named it Disillusion Island? she wondered, but she didn't dare to ask. Instead she said determinedly though a certain nervousness shook her
voice, 'You—you haven't told me anything about Warrianda, Mr Gascoyne.'

He glanced at her swiftly, and the qualities she knew
were back in his face—the harshness, the worldiness,
the cynicism.

'You'd better call me Steve,' he remarked. 'Your
cousin did. As for Warrianda, haven't you heard all
about it from Jan?'

'I've hardly heard a thing,' she admitted. 'We—we
shan't be alone, shall we?'

She flinched at his mocking laughter.

'You don't even know that?'

'No, I don't,' she said shortly. She felt a fool and she
clenched her fists angrily. 'Who else lives in your house
now your aunt's—gone?' she asked as he didn't offer
any information. She hoped she wasn't letting herself
in for some mammoth task, like feeding a mob of men
every day. Though if she had to do it, then she would.
She had to resist a sudden inner impulse to say, 'Take

me back—I don't want to come after all!' It was hardly
something you could say to someone who was piloting a
small plane.

'My brother Charles and his wife,' she heard him
telling her briefly, and she felt a new shock of surprise.
Why should anyone be needed to do housekeeping if
there was already a woman at the homestead? Before
she had a chance to ask him that question, he added,
'I'll be introducing you as my fiancée, by the way.'

'You certainly won't!' she exclaimed indignantly,
unable to believe her ears. 'I haven't agreed to that, and
you know it. You—you said you were offering me a
different proposition—that it would be the way I
wanted it.'

'I have offered you a different proposition—and it is
the way you wanted it, more or less,' he said infuriat-
ingly. 'The original idea—and I thought it was yours
too—seemed to be that you should be my wife and
share my bed.' He glanced at her, his dark brows
raised. 'I've excused you from marriage, haven't I?'

She met his eyes and her cheeks grew hot. '*And* from
—from——'

'Sharing my bed?' he finished for her. 'Well, there's
a spare room at the homestead.'

'You talk about *women* cheating,' she muttered between her teeth after a long moment when wild
thoughts chased each other confusedly through her
mind. She had to get out of this—the whole thing was
becoming utterly preposterous. 'Your brother will
never believe you've got engaged again so soon anyhow,' she told him scornfully.

'Oh, I think he will. It was pretty obvious I had plans
to marry when Jan was around,' he said carelessly.

'You're utterly cold-blooded,' Ellis said after a moment.

'Do you really believe that?' He turned and looked fully into her eyes, and she felt her heart come into her throat. She knew very well what he was referring to, and a feeling of shame almost choked her, as she shrank away from a glance that somehow seemed to see her naked. 'Neither of us is exactly cold-blooded,' he said reminiscently. 'We'll have very little trouble convincing anyone of our ardour.'

'You're—odious,' she said in a low voice. 'But you're not getting away with it. I shall flatly contradict you if you say we're engaged.'

He smiled disagreeably. 'You think they're more likely to believe you're the new housekeeper, do you? Well, I don't know exactly how old you are, Ellis, but you look no more than eighteen or so, and in case you're not aware of it, you're a very sexy little thing as well, in your pretty dress, with your pretty legs and those long flirty eyelashes. I'd be deceiving you if I allowed you to believe you could persuade the population of Flinders that you're no more to me than a housekeeper.'

Ellis couldn't think of a thing to say. She didn't think she was at all sexy, but all the same she had the wit to realise there must be something in what he implied people would think about their relationship. For a mad moment she wished she had never allowed Jake to persuade her to go to the hairdresser, or to spend all that money on clothes for her. She wished she looked just the way she had when she was keeping house for Uncle Bill. All the same, she was not going to pretend to be engaged to Steve Gascoyne, not for any reason on earth, and that was that.

Rather desperately she looked through the window and discovered they were over Flinders Island. A narrow jetty reached out into the water—there was a group of tiny buildings. The town of Whitemark, for sure.

All too soon they would be landing, he would be saying she was his fiancée—they'd be paired off, and it would be taken for granted he had the right to kiss her, to be alone with her. She was filled with panic. It was worse than the way she felt when that black wave of despair crashed over her head at the remembrance of Paul.

She hadn't thought of Paul even once during this flight. That was a sobering and slightly shocking realisation.

Meanwhile the man beside her felt in his pocket and without even looking at her thrust something into her hand—a small, dark red jeweller's box.

'Your engagement ring,' he said coolly. 'I bought it this morning.'

Despite herself, she opened the box, then, as the fire of emeralds caught her eye, she snapped it shut again.

'What's the matter? I assure you they're real. I wouldn't attempt to trick you with cheap imitations, knowing your tastes. Put it on,' he concluded in the commanding tone of one who is used to being obeyed.

'You must think I'm mad—that I have no pride!' Ellis choked. She had a fair idea what she would be agreeing to once that ring was on her finger—what liberties he would consider himself entitled to take with her.

'I don't think you're mad at all,' he told her equably. 'As for your pride—well, how shall I put it?' She saw his mouth quirk. 'You might find it's quite something to be my fiancée.'

'And I might not,' she said swiftly. 'I don't want your ring.' She thrust the box towards him, and when he ignored her she leaned forward and deliberately dropped it on the floor. He ignored that too, and glancing at the hard implacability of his profile, she knew she was mad, that she should never have trusted him—

not after the way he had behaved in the hotel bedroom. He wanted a wife—he'd decided to have her in his bed, as he put it, by trickery if he could get her no other way. But it was not going to happen. He couldn't force her to a pretence she didn't want. She wouldn't wear his ring and she would stick to a policy of distance. She'd be a very cool and remote housekeeper, and it would soon be obvious she was very far from being enamoured of Steve Gascoyne.

A few minutes later, during which time neither of them said a word, Steve gestured for her to look below.

'Warrianda,' he said briefly.

Ellis looked through the window. A little ahead she saw a group of buildings, a network of white tracks. One of them, thicker than the others, led to a house that stood among trees. The homestead, she supposed, and knew that in other circumstances she'd have felt a thrill of excitement. But not now. She was merely tensed up. There were mountains ahead, and to the left beyond dark scrub there was a rugged coastline, though she could see the silver curve of a beach against the sparkle of the sea. A tiny vehicle came racing across a paddock, and Steve said, 'That will be my brother Charles. He's coming out to the landing strip to pick us up. You'd better brace yourself.'

'For what?' she retorted. 'I won't go through with this pretence you're trying to force on me. I'm the— the housekeeper, and nothing more.'

He smiled sceptically. 'If I tell Charles that, he's going to laugh in my face.'

Ellis's heart began to thump. The plane was coming down rapidly now, the ground was racing towards them, she could see the cleared strip where they were going to land, and she said no more. Steve brought the little plane down smoothly, touching down with scarcely a bump, then taxiing gently to a standstill. The jeep hadn't yet come into sight, and Ellis turned to him and said anxiously, 'You're not being fair, you know. All I contracted to do was the cooking—the housework —that sort of thing. Now you—you——'

His eyebrows tilted. 'Now I want you to wear a ring?' He had retrieved the small box from the floor and now he tossed it up and caught it and put it back in his pocket. 'I haven't asked anything else of you, have I?'

'Not yet,' she thought, mistrusting the expression in those green eyes as they surveyed her. Meanwhile, the jeep had come racing along, and she said coolly, 'I warn you, Mr Gascoyne, if you say I'm your fiancée I shall call you a liar——'

'At least call me Steve,' he said mockingly, and she felt oddly disconcerted.

Her cheeks were flushed and her composure practically non-existent a moment later as she climbed out of the plane and found herself confronting a husky-looking young man with light brown hair and grey eyes. Steve's brother, much younger than he was, and resembling him only in that he too had a wide mouth. But *his* mouth was good-humoured and entirely lacked the cynical twist that was so obvious in Steve's mouth. He smiled at Ellis and his eyes accorded her a brief and casual inspection before he stooped and peered inside the plane. As Steve came round to shake him by the hand he commented, 'I thought you were going to hunt up a housekeeper before you came back, Steve.'

Steve ignored the remark and Ellis bit her lip. She wanted to exclaim, 'I'm the housekeeper,' but she had the dreadful feeling that Steve was right—his brother would laugh. Charles Gascoyne's smile and his quick inspection of her had said very plainly, 'So Steve has another girl'.

Steve took Ellis by the arm. 'Ellis, this is my brother, Charles. This is Ellis Lincoln, Charlie. And don't worry about a housekeeper—Ellis says she's going to look after us. She's not anything like as useless as she looks.'

Charlie smiled again and said 'Hi, Ellis,' but she didn't think he was impressed—not the right way, at least, because he grimaced and remarked, 'With shearing coming up, Leanne's going to be cranky. You know she can't cope with that sort of a deal.'

'I can cook for the shearers,' Ellis interjected, before Steve could speak. She was annoyed to find her voice pitched nervously high, but she was even more annoyed when both the men ignored her and proceeded to unload the cases and a few packages from the plane and transfer them to the jeep. Seething inwardly, she tagged along behind. Obviously Charlie didn't see her as the new housekeeper, and she supposed he most likely thought she was romantically interested in his brother. In fact, he'd probably think she was *really* eager, the way she was offering to look after the shearers. She writhed inwardly and wondered if she'd have felt any worse if Steve had said she was his fiancée. The fact that he hadn't should have given her a sense of triumph, yet it didn't. Her position was now so uncertain and vague that Charlie probably thought Steve was a bit dubious about her and had brought her to Warrianda for a—a try-out.

She felt decidedly uncomfortable as they all installed themselves in the jeep, herself between the two brothers.

As they drove to the homestead the two men talked briefly and sombrely of the death of their aunt, and followed that up with some discussion as to whether the recent rain would delay the shearing at Mussetts.

'I reckon Bob got enough sheep into the shed to get them dried out—they'll be right,' said Charlie, then presently asked Ellis politely, 'Do you think you're going to like Flinders, Ellis?'

Ellis didn't know how to answer. If she'd come here on a job, she might have said a polite yes, and if she'd been in love with Steve she'd have said yes, too. Actually, she found the thought of living on this island a romantic one. She had thought, when she'd written her letter to Steve Gascoyne, the simple farmer, that there she'd be able to disappear into the blue—start a new life in a place so isolated that Paul and the past would be so far far away they'd become unreal. As it was— if Steve Gascoyne was here then somehow the place wasn't isolated, it was overcrowded. And it was the situation here that was the unreal one—so unreal she simply didn't know how to cope with it.

Meanwhile she hadn't answered Charlie, and Steve said laconically, 'I think you've got Ellis stumped, Charlie. After all, the girl's only just this minute set foot on the place, and it's probably not in the least like she expected. She has a bit of adjusting to do before she decides if she's going to like it or not.'

'Sorry,' Charlie said with a smile. 'Where are you from, Ellis?'

'From Melbourne,' Ellis said, and knew he must be wondering where and how she'd met his brother. But he didn't ask, he was too tactful. She was debating whether she should say she was Jan Webster's cousin when Steve asked abruptly, 'Where's Leanne?'

'Leanne? Oh, she went into Whitemark shopping,' Charlie said, sounding vaguely uncomfortable. They were driving along a white road that glistened with quartz, and at the end of it was the thicket of trees hiding the house Ellis had seen from the air. Steve didn't pursue the subject of Leanne, but when Charlie pulled up at the gates he let him get out and open them and told him when he came back to the driver's seat, 'You can drop us off in the drive, Charlie. Ellis and I will sort ourselves out.'

'Okay,' his brother agreed, and added, 'Sorry about Leanne, but you know how it is.'

'It doesn't matter,' Steve said briefly.

The house, when they reached it, was a complete surprise to Ellis. The thick trees—she-oaks and tea-trees with a scattering of picturesque 'blackboys' under them—ringed a wide clearing that had been made into a garden, and set in the midst of it was an unexpectedly attractive two-storied house. It was like coming on a house in the middle of a forest, Ellis thought, so hidden and secret and away from the world it seemed. It had a grey sloping roof and wide eaves, and enormous windows that from upstairs, as she discovered later, gave a view of the sea. A white quartz-gravelled drive circled a lawn and garden beds, where there were clumps of blue and white agapanthus flowers—the Star of Bethlehem—and belladonna lilies shone like pink lamps from among the trees. It was hard to realise that beyond the sheltering trees there were all those paddocks, stretching away towards wild-looking granite-topped mountains etched against a blue sky.

Charlie pulled up in the shade of a red-flowering gum, and Steve swung the door open and climbed out, followed by Ellis.

'Carry on with what you were doing, Charlie,' he said as his younger brother helped him carry their belongings and the other packages up the steps to where the front door stood open. 'I'll probably join you later.'

Ellis, waiting at the door, felt a tremor of apprehension as the vehicle completed its circuit of the drive and disappeared into the trees, leaving her very much alone with the man whose fiancée she had refused to be.

'Go on in,' he told her. 'The bedrooms are upstairs.'

Ellis hesitated, then turned quickly away from the expression she saw in his eyes and started up the stairway. It was of polished wood, uncarpeted, and the open treads made it look very elegantly light and airy. She said uneasily over her shoulder to Steve, who was following her with the bags, 'I'm sorry Leanne's not here. I—I suppose she didn't know we were coming.'

'She knew *I* was coming,' he said. 'But I don't warrant a welcoming party as far as Leanne's concerned. She and I have a few differences of opinion.'

'I don't wonder,' thought Ellis, and paused at the top of the stairway so that he could show her where to go.

'You'd better have the spare room,' he decided. 'Leanne won't have done anything about Aunt Constance's room.' He moved across the wide hallway whose handsome polished floor was partly covered with thickly piled moss green carpet. There were dark beams in the ceiling, and Ellis commented on them out of nervousness.

'Oyster pine,' Steve told her. He pushed open a door and gestured for her to go in, then followed and deposited her two large bags on the floor. She watched him cross the room and pull back the yellow quilted bedcover. The thought came into her head quite madly that he was going to drag her over to the bed and make love to her, and she felt her heart begin to pound.

He looked up and stared at her.

'What's the matter now?'

'N-nothing,' she stammered. 'What do you mean?'

'The look on your face. You've thought of something that's got you in a panic.'

'I—I——' She searched wildly for an explanation, because of course he'd only been checking to see if the bed was made up. But she could think of nothing and her eyes fell before his. She moved blindly and picked up one of her suitcases. She had the awful feeling he knew exactly what she'd been thinking. He reached out and took the suitcase from her and she felt his fingers brush against hers and caught her breath. 'I'd—better unpack,' she said, her voice low.

'Take your time.' He deposited the bag on top of a low sturdy-looking chest that looked as if it had been carefully and lovingly made by some pioneer of long ago, then he turned and looked at her.

'I hope you're satisfied with the middle course I steered just now—the concession I made you. Or should I call it a—compromise?' he concluded, his green eyes mocking.

She felt her heart give a leap of anger. He knew very well she wasn't satisfied. She was quite positive he'd deliberately made her position a dubious one and her distrust of him deepened. She told him tartly, 'I'm not satisfied at all. Why should I be? Charlie was expecting you to bring a housekeeper, and you just ignored me when I said what I did about the shearers. You—you made me look a fake!'

He shrugged negligently. 'How do I know you're not? I didn't satisfy myself on that point last night . . . As for the housekeeper my brother was expecting, that's another story. In any case, as you already know, I'd sooner see you as my wife than anything else.'

She crimsoned slowly. 'I have no intention of becoming your—wife. Marriage is a—a serious business. You can't go into it with your eyes shut.'

'I certainly wouldn't do that. My eyes are well and truly open, Ellis. I gave up fantasising about love long ago.'

'You mean you don't believe in it, I suppose.'

He narrowed his eyes. 'I believe in love about as much as I believe in Father Christmas. It's a lot of makebelieve, and marriage is the same kind of a game.'

'Then it's a game I wouldn't care to play with you,' she said swiftly.

'At least you could be sure I wouldn't cheat,' he mocked. 'Well, make your bed. There's linen in the cupboard at the head of the stairs. Get unpacked. Feel free to look around the house and open all the doors. There are no secrets for you to discover. And tonight, by the way, Leanne will get the dinner, so keep out of the kitchen ... I'm going to change and get out in the paddocks with Charlie.'

When he had gone Ellis stared after him feeling frustrated and angry. Did he imagine she—or any girl at all—would agree to marry him when he didn't even pretend to any tender feelings?—when he said marriage was a game of makebelieve? Yet Jan had agreed to marry him, and Ellis couldn't for the life of her imagine why. Had she thought he was in love with her? And was he? Or—or couldn't Jan distinguish between love and passion? Certainly Steve Gascoyne was capable of passion——

Ellis put her two hands to her flushed cheeks and looked across the room at the big windows that had a view over the trees to the blue of the sea. Then, for the first time, she really looked at the room that had been given to her. Everything looked very comfortable and in the best of taste—the bed with its yellow cover, the pale floral curtains at the windows, the soft golden beige floor rugs. The furniture was dark and sheeny and looked so solid and old it must surely belong to the old pioneering days. Perhaps the Gascoynes had been pioneers. She didn't know, and, she reminded herself, she didn't care.

It was hardly a room for a housekeeper, she reflected wryly. From the size of the bed, it was a room for a man and his wife.

What kind of a room did Steve sleep in? she found herself wondering, and she knew that when he had left the house she would do as he had said—look into all the rooms, find out if he had a narrow monklike bed or—or a bed wide enough for sharing.

Good heavens, what mad thoughts she was having! With a feeling of guilt she attacked her suitcases, and began stowing her clothes away in the drawers and the wardrobe. All the lovely clothes Jake had heaped on her, some of them still unworn, unfamiliar, to help to mend her broken heart. Most nights at the hotel she had cried herself to sleep, but today she had barely thought of Paul. A new environment, new faces—but the simple fact was she had been too bothered by what she was doing, by her growing mistrust of Steve Gascoyne, to think of anything else at all.

She didn't look in the other rooms after all. While she was still in the midst of her unpacking she heard Steve go down the stairs and a few minutes later a car started up. Thank goodness he was out of the house, and she could relax, she thought. She finished her unpacking and then made up the bed, then found the bathroom and tidied up, though she didn't change out of the dress she was wearing.

She was brushing her hair at the mirror and trying to persuade herself that things would work out when she heard the sound of another car, an old noisy motor this time, not a quiet one like Steve had driven. Possibly it was Leanne back from shopping in Whitemark, and if so, then she had better go downstairs and introduce herself—and thank heaven she didn't have to say she was Steve's fiancée! She wondered what Leanne would be like. Charlie had struck her as being a pleasant young man, so it was likely that his wife would be a nice girl—and they would have something in common if she and Steve had a few differences of opinion!

The girl she found in the kitchen was a very slim, very young-looking girl with thick red wavy hair that reached below her shoulders, and a pale narrow face. She wore pale blue pants and a matching top in fine cotton that looked expensive—about the same quality as the clothes Jake had bought for Ellis, and she was somehow not in the least like a country girl who lived on a sheep station. She was busy over a big box of groceries on the kitchen table and she looked up and stared as Ellis appeared.

'Oh, where did you spring from? Are you—are you Bob Mussett's niece?'

'No, I'm Ellis Lincoln.' She added awkwardly, 'You —you wouldn't have heard of me. You're Leanne, aren't you? I—I came back with Steve.' She paused and wished she'd said Mr Gascoyne instead of Steve, and that she could somehow make herself say the unconvincing words, 'I'm the new housekeeper'. Yet she knew Leanne would laugh too—just as Charlie would have laughed.

Leanne's eyes widened fractionally, but all she said was, 'Oh, you're a—a friend of Steve's! That's nice ... Actually, we were expecting a housekeeper, and I thought I'd stock up the cupboards for a good start. Did she come with you?'

'No, I—there's just me,' Ellis stammered. 'I'm— I'm used to doing things——'

'Oh, for heaven's sake!' Leanne looked annoyed. 'You're not used to cooking for shearers, are you? He's got someone coming in a day or two, hasn't he?'

'No one else. I—I can manage.'

'Don't be mad. Why should you, when you've been asked on a visit?' Leanne was thrusting the groceries higgledy-piggledy into the cupboards now, and watching her, Ellis longed to take a hand and set them to rights. She wondered how long Leanne had been married. It was clear anyhow that she hadn't been capable of taking over when Steve's aunt had been taken to hospital, and presently she perched herself on the edge of the big table and asked Ellis, 'How long are you going to stay?'

'If you mean will I still be here when shearing's on,' Ellis said after a minute, 'I shall stay if—if I can help.' It seemed to her a diplomatic way to answer the question, because she would stay if she were here to work, and not as a guest, and she was determined to win her battle over that point. She might not like Steve Gascoyne, she certainly couldn't understand him, but she would work for him, and this was certainly a beautiful kitchen. There was a gas stove as well as a slow combustion one, a big fridge and a freezer, copious cupboards, and this massive table. There was even a dishwasher, she noticed.

Leanne digested her answer in silence, then offered her cigarettes and as she lit one for herself asked innocently, 'Have you known Steve long?'

'No, not very long.' She added, because Leanne expected her to say something, 'We met at the hotel in Hobart, as a matter of fact. I was—looking for a job and——' She stopped.

'And he asked you to come to Warrianda,' Leanne said with a knowing little smile. 'Well, Flinders Island is different from most places. It puts a lot of girls off.'

Off what? Ellis wondered. Off marrying Steve? But she didn't need to be put off.

Leanne slid off the table and wandered aimlessly to the door and looked outside into the sunshine. 'I can think of other places I'd rather be,' she said restlessly, then changed the subject to remark, 'Well, now there's no housekeeper, I'd better think about dinner. It's an awful bore. Charlie's aunt ran the house before, then she was ill and had to go to hospital. She died a few days ago.'

'I know,' Ellis said sympathetically. 'Steve told me. I suppose you miss her very much.'

Leanne shrugged and came back to the table. 'I didn't really know her all that well. Charlie and I have only been married three months—not quite that—and we had a month's honeymoon in Victoria before we came here. Aunt Constance was here then, and she did everything, so it wasn't too bad. Now it's hopeless. I haven't got the hang of this kitchen yet, and the slow combustion stove drives me crazy. I won't be able to cope with the shearers and I'm just not going to try. I really do think Steve might have brought someone back to *do* things.'

'Don't worry, Leanne,' said Ellis, relieved to find a housekeeper really was needed. 'I can do things, and if you like I'll get the dinner tonight to start with.' Steve had told her Leanne would do it, but wasn't it best to start the way she meant to go on? Leanne at any rate looked pleased enough.

'All right. If you're sure you want to.'

'I do,' Ellis said firmly. 'So don't you worry a bit. You'll be surprised how I can find my way round this kitchen ... What time do the men like to have their dinner?'

'Seven thirtyish,' Leanne told her. 'When they come in they like to have a wash up and a drink. Charlie likes a can of beer, and Steve usually has a whisky. There's some steak in the fridge,' she added. 'We don't eat lamb all the time, thank goodness. Are you sure you can manage? I'd really love to shower and change before Charlie comes in. I always feel so filthy after driving that horrible old car in to Whitemark.'

'Go ahead then,' said Ellis. 'I'll be all right.'

At the door, Leanne turned to tell her, 'I always dress up for dinner. At least we can pretend to be civilised, even if we're not.'

She vanished, and Ellis thought, 'She doesn't like it here,' and wondered why not—apart from the fact that she didn't seem capable of the work, which, apart from shearing time, surely wouldn't be oppressive. In Ellis's mind, the homestead was a very civilised one, and Steve, at least at the hotel in Hobart, had appeared to be a very civilised man, if dressing for dinner had anything to do with it. His attitude towards women, she had to admit, was little short of barbarous.

For the next little while she occupied herself quite happily finding her way about the kitchen, and doing a little swift reorganising of the cupboard shelves. She prepared vegetables and took the steaks from the refrigerator to take the chill off them before she cooked them. She located the dining room—a beautiful rather narrow room with one wall made completely of glass, looking through the green leaves of vines on to the side garden. There she laid the table, which she first covered with a gorgeous red linen cloth she found in the sideboard. All the cutlery and china and glassware were of high quality, and there were teak plates that she decided were used instead of table mats.

It was a charming house, and she only wished that its

owner was half as charming.

With everything prepared, she glanced at her watch and went quickly upstairs. Leanne hadn't reappeared, but the bathroom was unoccupied and she decided to take a shower. She laid out on the bed the outfit she had decided, after a little thought, that she would wear. She wasn't going to dress up. No, she was the house-keeper, and to remind Steve Gascoyne of that she'd wear her office-girl blouse and the black skirt.

As she laid it out on the bed she tried not to remember what had happened last night when she'd worn that blouse. The memory very nearly unnerved her, and quickly she departed for the bathroom.

CHAPTER FOUR

WHEN she came back to her room the wall lamp was on and Steve was there, rough-looking, almost a stranger in his checked shirt and tight cord pants. Ellis stood stock still in the doorway, clutching together the folds of her dressing gown that she'd belted carelessly in her hurry to get back to her room and dress.

'What's this in aid of?' he demanded, his eyes glittering.

As he was standing over the clothes on the bed, she couldn't pretend not to know what he was talking about.

'It's what I'm going to wear to dinner,' she said, her voice cold but her cheeks hot. The wardrobe door was open, and she knew she hadn't left it like that, so he must have been looking over her clothes, and as she came into the room he moved towards it.

'You've got a whole closet full of finery. Will you find something more suitable for dinner, or shall I?' He pulled a long-skirted green and ivory muslin dress free of its hanger and tossed it on to the bed. 'How about that thing? It will match your ring.'

'What ring?' she said, freezing.

'This ring,' he said, and took the box from his pocket.

Ellis stepped back a pace. 'I'm your housekeeper, Mr Gascoyne, in case you've forgotten, and I—I'll wear what I please. I'll be putting on that big apron I found hanging in the pantry when I go downstairs, anyhow.'

'Oh no, you won't. Leanne will be in the kitchen tonight.' He crossed the room to slam the door shut,

then came to face her, his eyes hard as they looked
down into hers. 'I told you when I left you this afternoon that Leanne would get the dinner, and I meant
it. What have you been doing? Taking charge while
I've been way? And exactly what did you tell my sister-
in-law?'

'What about?' she prevaricated, shivering inwardly.

'What do you think?' He was no more than fifteen
inches away from her and he took her roughly by the
arm as if he wanted to shake her. She could feel her
gown slipping and she clutched at it anxiously, her
heart hammering. 'About us, of course. About you and
me.'

'Nothing. There's—there's nothing to tell. I—I just
said I'd come with you,' she stammered, angry and
frightened at the same time, and thinking what a fool
she'd been to come here with a man of whom she knew
nothing. No wonder Jan had broken her engagement
if he'd treated her like this! Yet she knew he wouldn't
have treated Jan like his. He'd have made love to her,
and she would have let him—just as she was letting
Paul make love to her. But her morals weren't Ellis's
morals. The fact was, Steve was a fantastically handsome man, if you could get past the cynicism, the bitterness in his face. He had money too, that was obvious.
But none of that meant anything to Ellis, whatever it
had meant to Jan.

'I hope that *is* all you said,' he commented, letting her
go. 'You didn't, by some slip of the tongue, tell her you
were my new housekeeper?'

'No, but I wish I had,' she retorted defiantly. 'And
I did tell her I'd look after the shearers—if I'm still
here. It's not very fair of you to leave everything to
Leanne, especially when you promised you'd bring
someone back, anyhow.'

'I don't make promises of any kind to Leanne,' he said abruptly. 'She's one of those women who likes to carry the stockwhip, but I assure you she's not cracking it around *my* head. I'll get a new housekeeper in my own good time.'

'You've got me,' Ellis pointed out.

'I'm not interested in you in that way. You can do your little bit around the homestead, but I've told you what I feel about you.'

'What you *feel* about me?' she jeered. 'You—you don't feel anything.'

'I want a wife,' he said.

'I can't help that. Why should it be me?'

'Why not?' He looked at her through half-closed eyes, and she was aware of a sort of tensed-up menace from him. She backed away till she was near the chest of drawers. He didn't move, but he didn't take his eyes off her.

'You're available,' he said cynically after a moment. 'You've been—disappointed in love. I think that's the phrase. You offered yourself in that letter you wrote to me. Remember? And now you're here. That's why you.'

Ellis listened feeling her heart would leap out of her breast, its beating had become so agitated. She *was* here —and that was what was so inexplicable. She couldn't even explain it to herself. She couldn't understand how she'd been so gullible as to let him persuade her it would be all right, though when she thought of it, he hadn't actually done any persuading. He had flipped his fingers and she had come like the proverbial lamb —to the slaughter. She stared at Steve, her blue eyes wide and fearful, and she saw his long mouth curl upwards at the corners.

He said, 'I want you because your looks please me,

Ellis. Your voice pleases me too, when you're not spitting at me like a little cat. Quite apart from that, you have me persuaded that you're not purely ornamental. What more could a man want from a woman?'

'Am I expected to feel flattered?' she demanded. 'I'm really beginning to understand why Jan sent back your ring. You're—you're hardly any girl's idea of the ideal husband, Mr Gascoyne.'

'Call me that just once more and I'll make you sorry for it,' he said very softly. 'Who's *your* ideal, anyhow, Ellis? The man who's doubtless now making love to my ex-fiancée?' He paused and she said nothing. 'I don't believe *he* set any fires alight in you—you're still a very frightened little virgin, aren't you?—hugging your robe around you as if I were about to ravish you ... Or is your ideal more along the lines of the old family friend who was consoling you so lavishly in Hobart? If you knew just a little more about the human male, you might be glad I've delivered you from *his* clutches. He'd barely begun to—play with you so far, is my guess, and believe me, you'll be a lot better off with me. A man his age is usually motivated more by lust than by passion when he gets a pretty little innocent like you down on his couch.'

Ellis felt herself go white, but her eyes were blazing. She longed to smack this man in the face, but she hung on to her temper somehow as she stammered out, 'Don't you dare to speak about Jake like that! We—we don't have that sort of relationship. He—he's a good man. You're a warped character, Mr Gascoyne. You're the last man I'd ever want to—oh!'

The rest of her sentence was lost as with a sudden movement he reached out and crushed her against the hardness of his body.

'I warned you not to call me that,' he said into her

hair, and then he forced her head up and his mouth found hers.

She fought him this time, agonisingly conscious of the fact that she had not a stitch on under her robe and that it was no longer covering her nakedness anything like adequately. His mouth was bruising hers cruelly and she felt the strength of his hands as they pressed against her naked rib-cage so that she was rendered utterly helpless. She wanted to scream, but she hadn't a hope.

Then Leanne's voice shocked her by calling, 'Ellis, are you coming down to get the dinner? Oh!' Her exclamation of surprise was clearly audible because she had pushed open the door and was staring open-mouthed at the two figures still twined together.

'Go to hell, Leanne,' Steve gritted, without releasing Ellis. 'See to the dinner yourself——'

Leanne disappeared like magic, closing the door swiftly and silently behind her.

Ellis wrenched herself free of Steve and turned her back on him, wrapping her robe around her with fingers that shook.

'You're—you're detestable,' she muttered, swallowing on a sob. Her whole body was burning with shame. 'You—you shouldn't have come into my room——'

'You're damned right, I shouldn't,' he agreed harshly. His breathing, she noticed, was as uneven as her own. 'You'd better get dressed. I'm going to take a shower—a cold one.' From the door he told her wearily, 'Wear what you like,' and then she was alone.

'Wear what you like.' The words rang mockingly in Ellis's ears, as she stared at the clothes lying on her bed. What was the point in the black skirt, the office-girl blouse—the housekeeper's guise—*now*? Leanne would have no illusions as to why she was here: Steve

was on the warpath—he was looking for a wife and he'd
marked Ellis down.

She moved away from the bed and without knowing
what she was doing took up her brush and began to
draw it through her hair, her eyes fixed on her reflection. She felt so terrible she wished she could vanish—
that the girl with the golden-brown hair was simply
not there—that there was no image at all in the mirror.
Or she wished she could wake and find herself—oh
God, where? Somewhere back in her childhood, long
before she'd met Paul and been dropped by him, before
Jake had—gilded her—before she'd ever set eyes on
a barbarous man with black and silver hair who seemed
intent on——

As she tossed her brush down, she saw that he had
left the jeweller's box on the dressing table. She opened
it like one in a dream and slipped the ring on to her engagement finger. It fitted almost perfectly and its
emerald fires glittered hard and enigmatic as the green
eyes of the man who had left it there.

Ellis closed her eyes and bit hard on her lower lip.
Why should she feel so frightful about Leanne's having seen her in Steve Gascoyne's arms? But she knew
why—it hadn't been an ordinary embrace. Leanne
must have seen the state of her—undress, and she,
Ellis, was not the kind of girl who could simply shrug
it off. It hurt her self-esteem terribly to have Leanne
think she would let a man who was almost a stranger to
her take liberties like that. The old-fashioned phrase
coming into her mind made her wince, and she hated
the thought of having to face any of them again.

She took the ring off and put it back in its box, but
she knew she was madly tempted to leave it there on
her finger—to pretend to be engaged to Steve.
Wouldn't it be easiest that way? Then she wouldn't

have to fight him off—he would have a right to make
love to her within reason, to——

Ellis shivered, catching sight of her white and naked
body where the edges of her gown had parted. She
turned quickly away and looked around her as if she'd
just come out of a dream—a dream it shamed her to
remember. The room was growing dark despite the
light from the wall lamp, and she found the switch and
lit the little gold-shaded light that stood on the dressing table.

She couldn't stay hiding here all night, even if
Leanne was getting the dinner, and she tried to make
her mind a blank while she dressed, slipping on over
panties and bra the dress that he had chosen.

When she was ready, with her face carefully made
up, she had become a complete stranger. Paul would
never have known her, and neither would Jan or her
Uncle Bill. But Steve Gascoyne would recognise her.
She was the girl he had encountered in the Cabaret
Room at that sophisticated hotel in Hobart—the girl
with the elderly admirer, the girl another man had tried
to pick up. The girl who had sent out invitations with
her eyes, with her body.

That was the girl who was going downstairs to dine
in the gracious room with its red cloth and gleaming
silver and crystalware.

It's not me, Ellis thought exhaustedly.

She switched off her light and left the room. *She* was
the girl Steve Gascoyne wanted for his wife because she
was available, because she was there—because she had
written him a come-on letter.

And if she stayed much longer—oh yes, she would
marry him, because—because he would have com-
promised her. It was an unpalatable thought.

Joining the others downstairs was not, after all, the

nightmare she had imagined it might be. The sherry
Steve poured for her without consulting her taste—
dryish, light—certainly helped, as did the fact that the
lights were soft, and though she had coloured pain-
fully when she first came face to face with Leanne, the
other girl gave no sign that she even remembered what
she had seen. Ellis had expected a knowing smile at
the least, but none was forthcoming.

Later, it was Steve who went out to the kitchen to
give Leanne a hand with the steaks, and Ellis was left
alone with Charlie. They talked, but of what she afterwards had no recollection, though she was somehow
quite certain Leanne had said nothing to him about the
scene she had broken in on earlier.

As soon as she could after dinner, she excused herself, saying she was tired, and went upstairs to bed. She
was thankful Steve didn't offer to accompany her up
the stairs, but as she prepared for bed she wondered if
they were talking about her in the sitting room—asking Steve questions about her. Yet—she thought not.
Steve wasn't the sort of person who'd submit to being
questioned, and if he was, she had a pretty strong idea
he wouldn't answer.

She got into bed and lay in the dark, her eyes wide
open—sleepless, listening. But there was nothing to
hear, nothing at all. Nobody came upstairs, there were
no voices. She thought about the day that had just
passed and it seemed an eternity since she had first met
Steve. She knew him and yet she didn't know him, and
it disturbed her deeply to remember how he had kissed
her, and the emotions he had aroused in her. Sex, for
her, was something you reserved for the man you loved,
and yet her physical being had responded to him with
such ardour that even now she ached all through.

She closed her eyes and turned on her side and tried

to think of Paul, but for once she could barely call up his image, and the painful longing that always rose in her when she relived the tender moments she had known with him simply didn't come. Those tender moments seemed so pale and ghostlike and far away, whereas the memory of Steve Gascoyne's passionate approaches, that totally lacked any kind of tenderness, raged in her mind like some demon.

Sleep refused to come, and she wondered restlessly what tomorrow would bring. Whether she'd be able to start on some kind of routine of work in the house. Knowing that now Leanne had seen what she had, she couldn't possibly hope to be looked on as a house-keeper.

It seemed hours later that she heard movements in the hall outside her room, and she knew the others must at last have come up to bed. Yet still she couldn't sleep, and at last, in the silence, she slid out of bed, put on her slippers and her robe, and went softly along the hall and down the stairs feeling her way in the darkness. She'd heat herself some milk—anything to persuade herself she'd sleep, otherwise she'd be fit for nothing in the morning.

When she reached the foot of the stairs she saw a line of light under the dining room door and she heard voices. For an instant she stood petrified, and then she realised it was Charlie and Leanne talking, and that they sounded as if they were having some sort of an argument. Ellis hesitated, then went on towards the kitchen, and had a slight shock when she discovered the light was on. But no one was there and she proceeded to do what she had come to do, getting the jug of milk from the fridge and pouring some carefully into a small saucepan. She set it to heat on the gas stove while she found herself a heavy glass. It was curious, but in here, perhaps because the second door was open, she could hear the voices much more clearly, and she caught a few words without even giving her attention to it.

'Now you're being difficult.' That was Charlie, and Leanne's voice was raised as she snapped back,

'I am not! *You're* beginning to sound just like your marvellous big brother.'

'And is there anything wrong with that?'

'Plenty,' Leanne said shrilly. 'Seeing he thinks women are such second-rate citizens, only useful for breeding. You might try pleasing *me* sometimes just for a change instead of falling all over yourself to do what he says. I am your wife, after all.'

Ellis felt a pang of sympathy for Leanne even though she sounded rather waspish. She poured her milk and ran water into the saucepan, quietly so they wouldn't hear her and be embarrassed. She heard Leanne saying, 'No one expects *you* to be an unpaid shearers' cook. It's all very well telling me he'll get someone next time he goes to Tassie, but that won't be till *after* the shearing. Now will it?'

'I suppose not,' Charlie said, sounding uncomfortable. 'But you don't have to do your block. Ellis will help you—if you want to know, she said so herself when I went out to meet the plane.'

Ellis, on the point of taking her glass of milk upstairs, paused, and because her name had been mentioned, she actually strained her ears to hear what was said next. After all, she reasoned with herself, Leanne had burst in on her——

She heard Leanne laugh. 'How long do you imagine that'll last? She's more interested in Steve's lovemaking than in me or the shearers. She promised to get the dinner tonight, but she didn't. She was much too busy with your brother in her bedroom.'

Ellis's ears burned. Now Leanne was about to tell Charlie what she had seen, but he interjected sharply, 'All right, so I don't want to hear about it. I guess she's in love with him, and that's okay as far as I'm concerned.'

'Well, she's a nitwit if she thinks he's in love with her,' Leanne said. 'He only loves himself, as Jan Webster discovered. And I meant what I said, Charlie—I won't stay here. If you don't just tell Steve we're going to Koolong, I'll—I'll leave you.'

'Let's not go over all that, Leanne,' Charlie said wearily. 'You're unreasonable—you don't know what you're talking about, and I'm going up to bed.'

Ellis gave a guilty start. Heavens! Would he come to the kitchen to put the lights out? She didn't know what to do. She was going to suffer the indignity of being caught out, if she wasn't careful, and she glanced around her wildly, then quickly crossed the room and disappeared inside the pantry. After a minute, the light was switched off and there were sounds indicating that Leanne and Charlie were going upstairs. Ellis drank her milk in the darkness, groped her way to the sink and put her glass on the draining board. For some minutes she stood looking out at the garden where the tall blue and white lilies gleamed in the starlight. The thumping of her heart had settled down when at last she judged it safe to go up to her bedroom, though it wasn't until she was back in bed that she began to think about what she had heard.

First and foremost about herself, of course. Obviously, they both thought she was in love with Steve—was out to win him. The fact that Leanne was so sceptical about *his* feelings made it all the worse that she had seen Ellis, half undressed, in his arms.

But uneasy thoughts like these weren't going to

help her get to sleep, and she turned her thoughts to the place Leanne had mentioned—Koolong—and she wondered where it was, and whether Leanne had really meant it when she said she'd leave Charlie if he didn't take her there. They surely couldn't go away and leave her here alone with Steve! But if they did, of course she didn't have to stay. She wasn't a prisoner— she could leave any time she liked. She could telephone to Whitemark for a taxi—take the plane to Melbourne or Launceston the moment she wanted to.

And, in fact, she had half a mind to do just that to-morrow, and put an end to this whole crazy situation.

But she didn't leave the following day. She didn't even think about it. The world at breakfast time, with the sky so blue and clear and the sun already so warm, was somehow reassuringly normal. No one would guess from their manner that Charlie and Leanne had been quarrelling last night—and neither would anyone guess, she reflected wryly, from the casual, abstracted way Steve treated her, that she had been—wrestling with him in her bedroom the previous evening.

But of course, Leanne didn't have to guess. Leanne knew.

'You girls can do what you like today,' Steve said as he got up from the breakfast table after he and Charlie had demolished a large meal of chops and eggs. 'Why don't you take Ellis over to the beach, Leanne—take a picnic with you. You can forget about us—have fun.'

Leanne grimaced. 'Have fun—in that awful old bomb of a car that's all the Gascoyne family seems able to spare for me! It'll break down one of these days and I'll be stranded out there in the scrub with the snakes and the wallabies. We might as well stay home as usual and twiddle our thumbs.'

'Oh, Lee!' Charlie exclaimed, frowning. 'Don't be

so hard to get on with! You might as well go to the beach—you've got a beaut new swimsuit——'

'And there'll be no one to see it but the seagulls,' Leanne turned away and Ellis saw her mouth trembling. If Steve saw it too, he was quite unmoved, for without another word he disappeared. Charlie hesitated, then came around the table to kiss his wife, but she pushed him away. 'Go on—don't keep your big brother waiting.'

Abruptly, Charlie let her go and left the room. Ellis felt an uncomfortable witness. If she hadn't overheard that private conversation the previous night, she'd have been completely at a loss.

'What's up, Leanne?' she asked, beginning to pack up the breakfast dishes. 'Aren't you feeling well today?'

Leanne's eyes were smouldering. 'I'm just fed up with Steve pushing me around, that's all. Maybe you're the kind of girl who likes a man to order her about, but I'm not—particularly if he's not even my husband.'

'Oh, Steve wasn't really ordering you about, was he?' Ellis said reasonably—though she wondered why *she* should be championing Steve even remotely. 'He said we could do as we liked, didn't he?'

Leanne widened her eyes. 'And who is he to say *I* can do as I like? I'm married—I'm twenty-one—surely I can do as I like without having to get *his* permission. But you might as well know, Ellis, anyone who lives on this island with Steve Gascoyne hasn't a single solitary hope of doing what they like. They have to do what *he* likes. I don't even want to *live* here, but because Steve says so, here we are and here we stay. And now, as if that wasn't bad enough, I'm expected to do all the things Aunt Constance used to do. Well, I can't and I won't—and that's something he's going to find out very shortly.'

Ellis didn't know what to say. It was impossible to insist that Steve had brought *her* here to do the things Aunt Constance used to do. Leanne simply wouldn't believe her, not now she had seen Steve grappling with her in her bedroom. Finally she said mildly, 'I know I didn't do as I said and—and get the dinner last night, Leanne, but I am used to managing a household, and —and you can really leave things to me.'

'I have a good mind to do exactly that,' snapped Leanne. 'I'll show Steve Gascoyne! It was all very well for an old person like Aunt Constance—she was on all the committees that exist, she was even on the council for a while, but that's not my thing—I'm young, I'm not sixty or seventy or however old she was.'

Ellis took up a pile of dishes. 'Where would you like to live, Leanne?' she asked.

'At Koolong, of course.' Leanne actually looked surprised at the question, and she too took up some cups and saucers and followed Ellis out to the kitchen. '*There*, I wouldn't be expected to traipse around in an apron with a duster in one hand and a pile of dirty dishes in the other and—and a load of washing on my head. There's someone to do all those things at Koolong. The women can *really* please themselves what they do.'

Ellis listened thoughtfully and then said hesitantly, 'I'm afraid I don't know where Koolong is. Should I?'

Leanne blinked. 'What? You mean you really don't know about Koolong? You've never heard of it?'

'No,' said Ellis mystified. 'You'll have to enlighten me.'

'Well, Koolong and the Gascoynes go together,' Leanne explained, raising her finely pencilled eyebrows. 'Koolong *is* the Gascoynes. And you've never heard of it!'

'No, I haven't, Ellis repeated, a little irritated. She added, 'I've never mixed with country people.'

'Then you're starting at the top,' Leanne told her. 'Koolong's in the Goulburn Valley in Victoria, and it's a sheep stud as well as producing the best Merino wool. Everyone who knows anything about sheep has heard of Koolong. There's the most beautiful old homestead on the property with absolutely everything modern inside.' She perched on the edge of the table and picked at the polish on her nails while Ellis got on with the work. 'There's a swimming pool and a tennis court and a ballroom—*and* a billiard table. And plenty of staff to do the work. They have parties there all the time, and you can go for a holiday in Melbourne or Hongkong or wherever you want. Anytime,' she added. 'It's fabulous. They were having a second house built when I was there with Charlie on our honeymoon —for Diana and Christopher. Diana's Charlie's sister,' she explained, seeing the question on Ellis's face. 'She and Chris were married not long before we were.'

'And—Warrianda——' Ellis began, and paused.

'Oh, the old grandfather bought this place when Charlie's father took over at Koolong. He left it to Steve because he was the eldest or his favourite or something, I suppose,' Leanne said uninterestedly, pushing back her heavy red hair. 'Steve has a full share in Koolong as well, but he won't live there. He doesn't like it. He's a misanthrope, my mother says.' She suddenly widened her eyes and put a hand over her mouth. 'Oh, I shouldn't have said that, should I?'

'It's all right,' said Ellis, flushing and knowing what Leanne thought about her relationship with Steve.

'Anyhow,' Leanne resumed, 'what I mean is that Charlie and I should be living there, not here. Charlie doesn't get his full share of the income from Koolong till he turns twenty-five—that's in two years' time—but there's no reason why we should be roughing it with his big brother for—for peanuts in the meantime. It's unfair. Steve should pay someone else if he needs help, but Charlie won't see it. He can't grow out of the idea that he's the youngest in the family and must do as he's told. Steve doesn't like me,' she concluded, 'and this idea of doing without a housekeeper is the last straw.'

Ellis stacked the dishes in the dishwasher and remarked without turning round, 'I suppose you wouldn't believe it if I said I was the housekeeper, Leanne.'

She heard the other girl give a brief laugh. 'I'm afraid I wouldn't. It's obvious you're Steve's new girl-friend.'

Ellis said nothing. To contradict would be to lay herself open to giving all kinds of lengthy explanations, and she sighed inwardly and was trying to think of some way of changing the conversation when Leanne added, 'I suppose I shouldn't have told you about Koolong since Steve hasn't.'

'What difference does it make?' Ellis looked at her in surprise.

'Well, Steve will never live there.'

'So what?' Ellis wanted to say, instead she asked mildly, 'Why not?'

Leanne shrugged. 'I haven't a clue. Charlie's never said. He used to live there—he and Colin, that's the second eldest, helped their father run the property. I don't know why Steve got out, but I do know he's got this kinky idea that Warrianda's the only place in the world. That and a little island he owns where he runs cattle.'

'Disillusion Island,' Ellis said slowly. 'Yes, he pointed it out to me when we flew over.'

Leanne shuddered. 'What a name! I've never been there and I never want to go, though it can't be much worse than here. I never dreamed I'd be incarcerated here when I married Charlie. Pretty soon he's going to decide who he really wants to please—me or his brother.'

Ellis made no comment. It didn't seem very fair that Charlie should work on his brother's property for a mere pittance—for peanuts, as Leanne had said. Yet while she could well imagine Steve forcing his will on other people, Charlie didn't strike her as being exactly a weak character. Perhaps he was not as keen as his wife to live at Koolong, and she tried to remember what he had said last night. It was certainly Leanne who had been insisting he should tell Steve they were going to Koolong.

As if to settle the point, Leanne said moodily, 'We spent two glorious weeks of our honeymoon on Koolong. I honestly thought we were there to stay. Charlie and I are both gregarious—we love lots of people and parties. Then Steve flew up and spoilt it all. Next thing, we were dumped here and we've been here ever since.'

Ellis decided not to sympathise but to remain neutral. Their problems weren't hers, and anyhow, the housekeeper shouldn't get involved in personalities. After a moment she asked Leanne if she thought they should make a start on clearing up Miss Gascoyne's room.

'Steve said something about it yesterday, I think,' she concluded.

Leanne shuddered. 'It's not a task I fancy tackling. Dead people's things—I think someone belonging to the family should do it—such as Diana,' she added.

Ellis remembered when her own aunt had died. Jan hadn't done a thing about sorting out her effects, and young though she was, she had done it alone. Now she said, 'I'll talk to Steve about it. If he wants it left to his sister then we'll leave it, but if not, I can manage.'

Leanne gave her an odd look but didn't offer to help. It seemed to Ellis that she was stubbornly determined to do as little as she could.

Presently they both went upstairs to tidy their bedrooms. Leanne hadn't said a word about going to the beach, so Ellis said nothing about it either, and when she had finished her room she cleaned the bathroom, then after a slight hesitation decided to tidy Steve's room.

It was, as she suspected, the room furthest from her own, and the minute she stepped inside she caught the scent of his after-shave lotion. She knew it almost sickeningly well. It had been in her nostrils when he took her in his arms in Hobart. His room looked tidy and he had made his bed—a bed quite decidedly wide enough for sharing. She stood staring at the quilted cover with its diamond pattern in bronze and gold and off-white, feeling her heart beating hard. It was a very masculine room, a little austere. There were no photographs—a row of books on a low shelf, a bedside clock, pewter-backed brushes on the dressing table. Almost tiptoeing, Ellis collected two shirts that had been flung down on a chair. They'd need washing——

She'd come in from hanging them out on the line when she encountered Leanne again, and the other girl looked at her exasperatedly.

'For heaven's sake, have you been washing Steve's shirts? I'd have stopped you if I'd known. If he runs out of clothes he might start to realise what it means to have no housekeeper around.'

'It was no trouble,' Ellis said, more than a little embarrassed. 'And haven't you been—been doing the laundry since Miss Gascoyne went to hospital?'

'Not for Steve. We had a woman over from Launceston for a couple of weeks, but she didn't like it here and she left just before Steve flew down to Hobart. This will be his first real taste of doing without and I don't intend to make it easy for him. He doesn't go out of his way to make things easy for me.'

Ellis said no more. The men didn't come home for lunch, and she made a salad which she and Leanne ate sitting in the shade in the garden. Then Leanne announced that she intended to bring out a recliner and a book and have a rest.

'I hardly slept last night. I was fuming over Steve.'

'No drive to the beach?' asked Ellis.

'What's the point?' was Leanne's answer.

Ellis did the washing up and went upstairs feeling rather useless. She was disappointed in Leanne. They could have had some fun together, but it seemed Leanne was intent on sulking. In her room, she wandered across to the dressing table and with a slight shock discovered the small red jeweller's box still there. She picked it up and looked at the ring without taking it out. *He'd* bought it for her the day they'd left Hobart. Had he really imagined she'd accept it, wear it, after what she'd said? She stood thinking about him, her feelings oddly confused. He had a considerable amount of charm—but he was so hard! It was easier to hate him than to love him. And she had felt sorry for him! That was laughable.

She looked up, drawn out of her reverie by a sound, and through the mirror she saw Leanne had come to the door. The two girls smiled at each other warily. Ellis was thinking of last night and possibly Leanne was too, and now she came across the room.

'Look, Ellis, why don't you take the car and go to

the beach?' She stopped suddenly and Ellis realised with a start that she had without realising it slipped Steve's ring on to her finger. Her face flooded with colour and she pulled it off and put it back in the box. She said jerkily, 'I'd like to take the car. Do you—do you know where I'd be likely to find Martin Webster?'

Leanne looked at her so blankly she almost laughed.

'Martin Webster?' Leanne repeated stupidly.

'He's my cousin,' Ellis said awkwardly.

Leanne's face reddened. 'Then you—you know about Jan?'

'Yes. That's how I came to meet Steve. I knew he—needed someone.' She broke off hopelessly and said instead, 'Where would I be likely to find Martin, anyhow?'

'He may be somewhere around North East River,' said Leanne, looking rather speculative. 'Charlie went fishing with him last weekend and that's where he was then. There are a lot of birds up that way, I believe. Isn't he doing something about birds?'

'Yes, he's a naturalist,' Ellis said briefly. 'Is it far to North East River?'

'Nowhere's far on this island,' Leanne said discontentedly. 'You'll have plenty of time to get there and back before dinner time, but he mightn't be there.'

'I'll take a chance,' Ellis decided.

CHAPTER FIVE

A QUARTER of an hour later she was on her way and she was beginning to understand why Leanne made such a fuss about this car. It was an absolute bomb. The steering was bad, and the gear change difficult, and the engine sounded very sick. Ellis closed the gates carefully behind her as she drove through the Warrianda paddocks, and though she saw plenty of sheep she didn't catch a glimpse of either Charlie or Steve.

Leanne had told her to turn left outside the main gates, but as she drove along the lonely white road she began to have serious doubts about going to see Martin. She hadn't written to her uncle that she was on Flinders, and the more she thought of it, the more certain she felt that she didn't want Jan to know. It would seem so odd. And of course it *was* odd. Jan would imagine she was chasing Steve—and she would probably find that very funny because a man like Steve Gascoyne would never even look at a girl like the Ellis Lincoln Jan knew.

Ellis drove more and more slowly. She knew now she wasn't going to look up Martin, though in time, since he was friendly with Charlie, he would certainly discover she was there. But Ellis didn't want it to happen yet. In any case, she might not stay here much longer. It all depended whether or not Steve accepted her on her own terms. If he was going to jump on her every time he got her alone, then she would have to leave, but if he behaved himself she'd stay—at least until she found something else to do.

She saw no more than one or two farmhouses as she drove along, enjoying the sight of the green grasses rippled by the wind, the distant line of granite mountains, and the picturesque clumps of native pines. Occasionally there was a dead wallaby by the side of the road and once she saw a snake wriggling across the white quartz gravel.

When she reached a narrow track that turned off to the left she decided to take it and see if it led to the beach. It wound along through clumps of tea-trees and scrub and presently, sure enough, Ellis found herself by the sea, and her spirits rose. It would have been lovely to picnic here at the beach, but it appeared no one was going to tell Leanne what she was to do, and if Steve said, 'Go to the beach', then that was the last thing on earth Leanne would do.

Ellis drove slowly along looking for a good place to pull up. The sand was starkly white and the sea was like jewels—emeralds and sapphires, she thought, and that thought conjured up another—a sapphire ring for Jan, an emerald one for Ellis. It was funny how all her thoughts seemed to lead her to a man she'd met so resently and didn't even like. Once, all roads had led to Paul, every lovely thing she saw she had wanted to share with him. Not that, in retrospect, she had actually managed to share a great many of her thoughts or enjoyments with him. It was odd how thin that love affair was beginning to seem. It had consisted mostly of daydreams—of reliving his kisses, dreaming up love scenes —more passionate ones than ever eventuated.

What had Steve Gascoyne said? 'He didn't set any fires alight in you!' But he had, she thought, determinedly. She had been deeply in love with Paul.

Had been. It was a disquieting thought, and Ellis put it aside.

She pulled up under tea-trees on the slope above the beach. It was a small secluded beach that looked as if no one had ever visited it. There was not a footprint on the sand, not a boat or a human being in sight. Ellis climbed out of the car, relishing the quiet now the noisy motor had cut out, and made her way over clumps of coarse grass to the beach. The water looked so terribly inviting she wished she'd brought her swimsuit. The sun was hot and she pulled off her shoes and wandered along the sand, occasionally stooping to pick up a shell or to let the water wash over her feet.

Presently she flung herself down on the sand and stared at the seagulls that were the only living things within sight, but soon the temptation to go into the water grew too much to resist. She took a long look around her, then, deciding she was completely alone and perfectly safe, she quickly discarded her clothes —white jeans and a scoop-necked cotton shirt, bra and panties.

She enjoyed her wallow in the sea, and didn't care in the least that her hair was going to need washing and resetting—she'd attend to that when she got home. She had no idea of the time—she'd taken off her watch when she washed those shirts of Steve's and forgotten to put it on again, but she had plenty of time to dry off before she dressed again, and she stretched out on a big time-smoothed rock—flat on her stomach, her head turned to one side so that her cheek rested against the warmth of the great ancient rock that seemed to have been made for lying on.

She had never in her life been in a place so solitary, so quiet, so—so benevolent. This was an enchanted island—an island that loved her.

In minutes, she was asleep ...

She woke with a little shiver, to realise she was cold.

She was in shadow and for a dizzying moment she had no idea where she was. She had been dreaming vividly, but now the dream had fled and memory came back. She rolled over and sat up abruptly to reach for her clothes—and to discover with a chilling shock that the shadow that lay across her was a human one. She drew up her knees instantly, hugging them to her to hide herself, and looked up, her blue eyes widening.

Steve Gascoyne stood looking down at her.

Ellis felt both frightened and outraged. There was a look in his eyes—dark, brooding, primitive—that made her want to run, to escape. But naked, she could run nowhere—not into the sea, not across the clumps of yellow grass and into the tea-trees, not back to the car at the far end of the little beach. All she could do was to sit there, as still as the rock on which she had been lying.

He didn't apologise and he didn't turn away; he stood where he was and looked at her, and then he said, 'You look very beautiful there against the rock. As beautiful as a legend. I'm almost persuaded to believe in love again.'

He dropped down on the sand and Ellis felt a shiver run through her, and hugged her knees to her more fiercely than ever. She could imagine too vividly the shock of being pulled helpless into his arms, he looked so dark and powerful. He must have been back to the house, for instead of the checked shirt and cord pants he had worn at breakfast time, he was now in a silky black shirt with a polo neck and black pants that accentuated his lean muscular maleness. The white streak in his hair looked so dramatic in this setting it was easy to believe he was some superhuman demon, and what he was saying was no help at all. Nor was the way he looked at her.

She said quiveringly, 'Please—go away.'

His heavy dark eyebrows rose and his long mouth curved in an ironic smile. 'Words straight out of a silent prayer,' he said mockingly. 'But I'm afraid I'm not going to disappear, Ellis. Why should I, when my —intentions are honourable, when I've asked you to be my wife and to sleep in my bed?'

'Go away,' she breathed again. 'Leave me alone!'

'When I've found you naked? Which I didn't expect to do, by the way. No, it's too much to ask of any man, Ellis. Don't you know, my little moonbird, that if you take off all your clothes and fall asleep on the beach, then you must accept the consequences?'

'There—there aren't going to be any consequences,' she got out, wishing desperately that at least he would stop looking at her. Certainly she was being as modest as she could, but when you were quite bare it was decidedly difficult, and she realised far too late what a fool she had been to imagine she was safe here. It was such a small island. And suppose someone else had come and found her here? Though to tell the truth she thought she'd have felt safer with any other man in the world than she did with Steve Gascoyne at this instant. He had been menace enough in civilised Hobart, but here on this island he seemed to have shed his thin veneer of polite conventionality, and she knew she could expect anything of him. Her desperate exclamation, 'There aren't going to be any consequences', was sheer bravado, and of course he knew it.

Quite suddenly she wanted to weep, and she shook her dark gold hair forward and rested her head on her knees.

'I'm going to take pity on you, moonbird,' he said after what seemed endless seconds. 'Get into your clothes. I'll go back to the car and wait for you.'

Ellis raised her head to find he'd got to his feet and stood looking at her, a crooked smile on his mouth. 'You're quite helpless, aren't you?' he said reflectively. 'That's something a woman does well to remember—her physical inferiority. I've only to take you by a handful of your beautiful hair and you'll be completely at my mercy. You might kick and scratch and call me names, but it would get you nowhere if I decided to make love to you, would it?'

'That would be—rape,' she said huskily but defiantly.

'It wouldn't be rape. I'm talking about making love,' he said.

She stared up at him and her pulses raced. Those strange greenish eyes seemed to have some supernatural power over her, and somewhere deep inside a voice told her that what he said was true. If he should start making love to her now—she wouldn't be forced into anything against her will. Once she was in his arms, with his lips on hers and his hands caressing her, she'd allow him to do as he pleased with her. She knew that from her experience of him already, and the thought frightened her. Her body had weakened before, when he took her in his arms, her principles had been all but decimated by her purely physical reaction to the male in him. She'd never felt the least like that with Paul, and yet she'd been in love with Paul. It was—it was crazy, and it was frightening.

She felt the tenseness leave her as he abruptly turned his back and walked away. Shivering, she reached out for her pitiful heap of clothes, thinking how ludicrously little could stand between a feeling of fear and one of security. Yet a few garments were certainly not going to protect her from Steve Gascoyne, particularly on this beach where she was completely and helplessly alone with him.

She fastened her bra with trembling fingers, pulled her shirt over her head and wriggled into her panties, keeping her eye on his retreating figure as she did so. With a final gasp of relief she got into her jeans, zipping them up as she straightened. He stood waiting for her now on the edge of the sand below where the two cars were parked, and clenching her fists she began to walk towards him. Steve watched every step she took as she picked her way across the dry white sand, her sandals in her hand. At least she didn't have to suffer the indignity of plodding, for the sand was firm and smooth under her feet, and if it hadn't been for Steve Gascoyne waiting menacingly ahead, she'd have enjoyed the sensual pleasure of it a whole lot more.

'They say that well chosen dress can arouse a man's desires more than nudity,' he said conversationally as she drew near. 'I'm undecided about that where you're concerned, Ellis. I've seen a good few naked women, but you, in a state of complete undress, I find distinctly dangerous.'

'Really? Well, I'm not interested,' she said stiffly.

'No? If that's so, then you're not human,' he said with a faint smile.

'All right—then I'm *not* human,' she retorted.

'Oh yes, you are.' His arm reached out and he whipped her body against his. Whether by accident or design she didn't know, but they both collapsed on the sand and she was wrestling with him, but he had captured her and held her helpless within seconds. He kissed her mouth, he bit her shoulder through the cotton shirt, his lips found the most sensitive part of her breast and despite the stuff of her clothes, she was aroused. She felt herself clinging to him, as her inhibitions gave way, and it was Steve who called a halt to the play with agonising abruptness. Ellis rolled away from him and scrambled to her feet, crimson-cheeked and undignified.

He got to his feet too and looked down at her mockingly. 'You're human all right—and it wouldn't be rape, would it?' he remarked, and fury cut through her.

'You're—odious—despicable! You're—you're like a cat playing with a mouse!'

'Perhaps I am,' he agreed after a moment. 'But you aren't quite like the mouse that's being played with. You were enjoying the game too, weren't you?'

'I was not,' she said violently, because he had hit on a truth of which she was utterly ashamed. 'I—I hate you even *touching* me. I *hate* you! All I want on this island is to——'

His hand covered her mouth smotheringly. 'If you mention that word I'm forcing you to swallow down just one more time, I think I'll throttle you, Ellis. You've been bleating it out all morning to Leanne, haven't you?—meanwhile washing shirts and cleaning bathrooms and busying yourself about the house like some industrious little domestic. It's no wonder you fell asleep on the beach. But you won't fool anyone, you know—not Leanne, and not Charlie.'

Ellis hated him all the more. She didn't understand how he could be embracing her on the sand one minute and the next, attacking her about something so mundane. Yet if she stopped to think, she shouldn't be surprised. It wasn't as if he felt anything more than sheer animal passion where she was concerned. His instinct was to mate, to have children, and from her angle he had a most unpalatable way of trying to persuade a woman to live with him. She was not to be won with tactics like those, yet what he had already persuaded her into she was far from certain. Tears stung her eyes and she had a strong desire to bite the hand that still covered her mouth. It was only by reminding herself that to do so could have drastic consequences that she managed to refrain. Steve Gascoyne clearly believed that might was right.

And on this island it looked as though it was. He already kept Leanne and Charlie here against their will.

She was staring at him furiously and he dropped his hand from her mouth.

'Why didn't you bite me?' he taunted, but Ellis didn't answer. She snapped out instead, 'You like to be the lord and master, don't you? I'm beginning to understand why you prefer to live here instead of in the Goulburn Valley. Here you can *really* have everyone at your mercy!'

He put a hand in his pocket and produced cigarettes and lit one unhurriedly. 'Such as who?' he asked as he shook out the match.

'Such as Leanne,' she flung at him. 'And—and your brother Charlie.'

His brows came down over eyes that glittered dangerously. 'So the confidences have begun. Well, let me tell you this—Leanne and Charlie are at liberty to leave this island at any moment of any day they like. And the same goes for you. I wouldn't lift a finger to stop any of you.'

'I don't believe you,' Ellis said flatly, though she felt somewhat nonplussed.

'And I don't damned well care what you believe. Are you having visions of yourself as a missionary, rescuing the oppressed and the downtrodden, by any chance? If so then I'm afraid it's not an aspect of your personality that I'm prepared to find particularly attractive.'

'And I don't damned well care what you find attractive,' Ellis said heatedly. In a moment she was going to burst into tears. She was shaking with nerves already, and she didn't think that a woman's tears would engender anything but contempt from Steve Gascoyne. She moved away from him. 'I'm going ho—back to Warrianda to—to——'

'To cook the dinner,' he said derisively.

'Yes. You hired me to do that.'

'I suppose I did. But since we got here, I've changed my mind. You're more stimulating in the role of woman than as anything else. In effect, I don't give a damn if we eat tonight or not. I'd rather the relationship between you and me was waxing and growing fat.'

'I'm afraid *I* find it wearing *thin*,' she said through her teeth, and she leaped up the sandy bank and reached for the safety of the car.

She had to wait till he'd started his car up and moved out of the way ahead of her before she could get going, and it wasn't long till he'd left her far behind.

When she arrived back at the homestead she found, to her chagrin, that Leanne, aided apparently by Charlie, had already cooked the dinner.

Mustering the sheep for shearing was in process for the next few days, and Ellis began to breathe more freely. Steve had stopped pestering her, and when she asked if he'd like her to tidy up his aunt's belongings, he had agreed, somewhat to her surprise. As well, she quietly took over most of the tasks about the house from Leanne, who was talking about flying over to Melbourne to visit her mother.

'Oh, Lee, not while shearing's on,' Charlie had protested when she mentioned it, and Ellis took it for granted that Leanne would stay. But obviously there was more to it than the idea of an ordinary visit, for the very day before the shearers were coming, Leanne packed up her bags and announced over breakfast that she was going. Charlie, who presumably knew already and had said whatever he had to say in private, was silent, and though Ellis thought Steve would have something to say for sure, he made absolutely no comment. She felt acutely uncomfortable herself, and didn't at all relish the idea of being left here alone with the two men. Yet Steve had been so unobjectionable since that evening on the beach that she really had no grounds for alarm.

Charlie came into the kitchen to speak to her before he left the house to begin work.

'Ellis, would you mind running Lee in to Pat's River to get on the plane this afternoon? I'd do it myself, but I can't afford to take time off today with shearing beginning in the morning'

'That's all right,' Ellis said pleasantly. 'I'll drive her there. Is she—is she staying away long?'

'I shouldn't think so. She's just a bit homesick,' Charlie said, though not very convincingly. 'We haven't been married all that long, you know.'

'She—she doesn't like it here very much, does she?' Ellis suggested tentatively.

'Only because it's different from what she's used to. And Steve doesn't handle her right. He's inclined to be hard on women.' He smiled as he said it, and Ellis could see he wasn't really making a criticism of his brother. She was not so tolerant herself. A new marriage should be helped along, and Steve's attitude was surely making difficulties. She asked on impulse, 'Why don't you take her to the other place the Gascoynes own—the one in Victoria?'

His frown told her he didn't really think it was her business, but he told her civilly, 'Steve needs someone here—and I can learn a lot from him. Don't you worry your head about it anyhow, Ellis, and don't feel too sorry for Lee, she'll have a great time in Melbourne and come back fighting fit. It's tough on you to be landed with the shearers, but Lee wouldn't be all that much help if she were here, I'm afraid. Anyhow, Steve seems to think you'll make out, and it's good experience, isn't it?'

Ellis coloured and glanced away to give some attention to the dishwasher. She knew what Charlie meant. Good experience if she were contemplating marrying Steve. She said a noncommittal, 'I guess so,' and thought rather guiltily of that emerald ring still lying in its box on her dressing table. She hadn't returned it to Steve, but not because she'd forgotten about it. She saw it there every time she went to the mirror. The fact was, though, that she didn't want to reopen the subject while Steve was leaving her alone. She didn't trust him, of course. Something was going to happen some time, but they would all be working so hard while shearing was on that she told herself she was safe for a while yet.

She took Leanne to the airfield after an early lunch and found her rather defiant. 'I've taken the wind out of Charlie's sails this time, he'll be running after me before I have time to turn round,' she told Ellis as they waited in the tiny administration building. He'll begin to see I really mean it about not staying at Warrianda. I'm just miserable here, and I know I'd be perfectly happy at Koolong ... Well, looks like it's time to go. Thanks for bringing me out.' She smiled briefly, then went to join the four other passengers who were making their way to the small six-seater plane that would take them on the hour and a half flight to Melbourne.

Ellis stood at the glass door ready to wave, but

Leanne didn't look back. Unlike Charlie, she hadn't apologised for leaving Ellis to do all the work, but that was excusable on the grounds that she was very much wrapped up in her own problems.

When the plane had taken off, Ellis went back to the old car rather slowly. This would be her last day of freedom, she suspected, until the shearers were finished, though so far no one had seen fit to tell her exactly what her duties would be. No doubt Steve or Charlie would brief her tonight, but just now—she decided to drive the extra few kilometres in to Whitemark. She could think of a few odds and ends she wanted in the kitchen, but mainly she wanted to enjoy her freedom—and to have a look at Whitemark.

It was a very tiny settlement, she soon discovered. The one hotel dominated the main street, and behind it were the sea and the jetty. Ellis parked the car and discovered a supermarket attached to a garage, and went inside to emerge some time later with butter, a tin of pineapple, a tube of toothpaste and a block of chocolate. Head slightly lowered as she came into the sunlight, she ran slap bang into her cousin, Martin Webster.

Ellis nearly dropped her purchases in her surprise, but it was nothing to Martin's complete astonishment. He stared at her for a moment, then hugged her briefly.

'Ellis! What in the name of fortune are you doing here? And what have you done to yourself?'

Ellis blushed vividly, remembering as he spoke how her appearance had changed. She was fond of Martin, and the sight of his familiar face, his untidy red hair and his friendly blue eyes made her feel just a little weepy so that she had to blink quickly.

Martin put his arm around her shoulders. 'Don't try to answer yet—let's find a quiet spot where we can talk.

That is, if you have a moment.'

'Yes—yes, I have.' She gestured towards the old car she'd parked at the kerb. 'I'll put this stuff in the car first.'

'Good lord!' he exclaimed. 'Doesn't that old wreck belong to the Gascoynes? Don't tell me Jan's around —she can't be. I had a letter from Dad only yesterday. Look, let's find somewhere fast. Come up to my room. I'm staying at the Hotel for a few days.'

Ellis shut the car door, her head buzzing with confusion. It was marvellous to see Martin, but what on earth was she going to tell him? He was going to think the whole thing very strange indeed.

Once in his room, he settled her in a chair and told her firmly, 'Now—give, young Ellis!' His blue eyes were full of admiration as he added, 'You've had something done to your hair, haven't you? In fact—you look so *bella-bella* I'd say you must be in love, if I believed all I read.'

'Well, I'm not in love,' Ellis said rather anxiously. Martin was thirty, but he looked so boyish he could have been twenty-two, and he was about the kindest man she had ever met. He used to help her with her homework when she was still at school, and later, when she took over the house, he did all sorts of thoughtful things to help. That was until he'd moved into a flat of his own, and nowadays, as he spent a lot of time away from Melbourne doing research, they didn't see a great deal of each other.

'Well, okay, whatever you say, but you're certainly looking very beauteous,' he asserted. 'Now tell me how come you're here on Flinders.'

'It's a—long story,' she said awkwardly. 'As a matter of fact I haven't let Uncle Bill know that I'm here yet —or Jan either.'

She paused and he put in, 'You mean you want me to shut up about it.' He looked at her thoughtfully. 'You're not doing anything you shouldn't, are you?'

'No, of course not,' she said defensively. 'It's just that —well, I mightn't be staying long. I'm—I'm house-keeping—for the Gascoynes. Temporarily,' she added. 'You know their aunt died?—the one who kept house for them?'

'Yes, I know that. Charlie told me so the other day. But how on earth did you get mixed up with the Gascoynes, Ellis? Dad said you'd gone off on a holiday with Jake Armour in Tasmania, since Jan was there to take over for a while. Aren't you going back home again?'

'I don't think so, Martin,' Ellis said briefly. 'It's time I got out and tried my wings in the big world.'

'I agree,' said Martin. 'But how do you come to be trying your wings here? Flinders Island is hardly the big world,' he continued humorously.

Ellis couldn't think what to say, and he leaned over and clasped her wrist momentarily. 'I'm sorry, kid. I'm being inquisitive. Don't tell me if you don't want to. One thing I do feel impelled to say to you, however— don't lose your heart to Steve Gascoyne. You're far too sweet a little pippin for a cynic like him.'

Ellis coloured so deeply she was agonised. 'I—I won't lose my heart, Martin. I told you, I'm keeping house, that's all. I'm too busy to fall in love. Shearing starts tomorrow—I'm looking forward to that.'

Martin looked carefully away from her crimson face, stretching his arms over his head. 'You're an astounding little beastie, Ellis, but I sure hope you're not going to be overworked. At least I know you won't be under-paid—the whole world knows the Gascoynes are roll-ing in money. That, if you didn't know, is why Jan winged her way to Flinders when I happened to men-

tion in a letter that there were Gascoynes here—one
of them unattached. I was stunned when she got herself engaged so rapidly, and I'd dearly love to know
what made her break it off ... Ah well, she's having
another love affair now—though this one hasn't got as
far as engagement rings yet, or I'd have been told the
glad news.'

Ellis's colour had subsided by now, and he looked at
her again, his blue eyes kind and thoughtful.

'You're not going to tell me anything more about
yourself?'

Ellis bit her lip. It seemed churlish not to give him
some explanation, but she couldn't possibly admit to
having written a—come-on letter to Steve. Nor could
she admit he wanted to marry her. She drew a deep
breath and said haltingly, 'It's all been a sort of chain of
events. I'd heard from Jan about Miss Gascoyne going
to hospital and then—Steve happend to be at the hotel
in Hobart when I was there with Jake. He'd come down
for the funeral and he was—was looking for a housekeeper.' She stopped, uncertain what to say next, then
said somewhat disconnectedly and not very truthfully,
'Jake thought it was a good idea. He—he didn't think
I should go back to Uncle Bill.'

She glanced at Martin through her lashes, and
though she didn't think he quite believed her story, at
least he was pretending to, for he nodded and said seriously, 'I see. Well, it's something that Jake knows.
Anyhow, if you should by any chance get yourself into
deep water, don't forget I'm here, will you? I'll be
going back to the mainland in a few weeks, but I'll keep
in touch. Okeydoke?'

'Yes,' she said meekly. 'Thanks, Martin, but everything's all right, I'm going to be far too busy to get into
trouble of any kind.'

He didn't ask any more questions, and presently they went downstairs to the lounge where he had a beer and Ellis had a lemon squash, and over it, he talked to her about the research work he was doing. At the moment he was concentrating on the white-bellied sea eagle, and she was fascinated though slightly repelled when he told her he'd seen one of the parent birds carrying a fairy penguin to the eyrie to feed its young.

'I'll be going back to North East River shortly,' he told her. 'If Charlie Gascoyne's coming over that way fishing during the weekend, get him to bring you along too, will you?'

'I'd like that,' she said. They indulged in a little reminiscing until Ellis happened to glance at her watch.

'I'll have to get back! I've a dinner to cook.'

Martin stood up at once. 'Then I shan't keep you . . . How do you get on with Charlie's wife?' he asked as they walked across the road to her car.

'Oh, fine. She's very nice,' Ellis said, and hated herself for being evasive. But she just didn't want to tell him she was, from today, on her own with the two men. Not that she wasn't perfectly safe.

But in her heart she knew she was not safe, whether Leanne was there or not. And if Martin knew how Steve had been behaving, he'd probably be after him with a shotgun.

At the homestead, Steve's car was already standing in the driveway, though she'd imagined he'd be working late this evening. She parked the car at the side of the house and hurried inside with her purchases, going straight through to the kitchen. In the doorway, she stopped short. Steve was there and on the table were two enormous boxes. Ellis glimpsed bags of potatoes and onions, loaves of wrapped bread, a pile of cans. She raised her eyes to his face questioningly, and, when his green gaze flickered coldly over her, she shivered involuntarily, as if scenting danger.

'You've taken your time,' he said icily.

Ellis blinked. 'What do you mean? I had some shopping to do in Whitemark.' She tipped out the few items she had bought on to the table and indicated the boxes of provisions. 'What's all this?'

'What do you think it is? Food for the shearers, of course.' He looked contemptuously at her purchases. 'Shopping like that hardly warranted a trip to Whitemark.'

'Maybe it didn't,' she flared, and forbore to mention that she'd been almost there when she took Leanne to the airfield. 'But I didn't know there was any law against it.'

'There's not,' he said, still coldly. 'But at least you might tell the truth as to why you went. I know damned well it wasn't to buy half a pound of butter and a tube of toothpaste.'

Ellis put her head up. 'Then you know wrong, because it was. I'm—I'm almost out of toothpaste. Besides, I wanted to take a look around. I've never been to Whitemark.'

Steve came round the table and took her roughly by the shoulders. 'You're protesting too much, I saw your car in town. You went to see Martin Webster, didn't you?'

Her face grew pale. 'What are you implying? He's my cousin!'

'I don't care if he is your cousin.' He was holding on to her so hard that tears came into her eyes.

'Let go of me, Mr Gascoyne. You're—you're hurting me!'

'I mean to hurt you. And don't start calling me Mr Gascoyne ... I don't take kindly to having my fiancée spend time in a hotel bedroom with another man. That's what I call cheating. You can count yourself lucky I didn't come in and carry you out forcibly.'

Her eyes widened. 'I'm not your fiancée—and I'm not cheating!'

'You're the woman I'm going to marry,' he said with a deadly intentness.

Ellis shook her head wildly. 'I'm not—I'm not!'

'You haven't returned the ring I gave you,' he said remorselessly. 'As far as I'm concerned, that's a tacit acceptance.'

'I don't see it that way,' she said, her cheeks paling. 'I don't—I don't want it. You can take it back any time you like. And now will you please let me go?'

'In just one moment,' he said, and swept her against him, his mouth finding hers.

She struggled to escape, then desisted as she was inexorably drawn against his maleness—so close she seemed welded to him. Her mouth was warm and bruised from his kisses that wouldn't let her breathe, and suddenly all the resistance went out of her. Fires were shooting probing fingers of flame all through her body to its most secret places, and when he let her go it was all she could do to stop herself from locking her fingers behind his neck and drawing him back to a moment that she longed to repeat, however ashamed it made her feel.

She said shakily, 'Now may I go?'

'You'd better,' he said meaningly, his glance trailing down her figure from her visibly heaving breast to her trembling thighs, and the look in his eyes made her move quickly. When she reached the door he said, 'After dinner I'm going to brief you on the duties of shearers' cook.'

'I'd rather Charlie did that,' she said promptly,

shocked once again by his abrupt return to practical matters.

'Your preferences don't come into it. *I'm* going to brief you, then I'll know exactly what you've been told.'

Ellis didn't answer that. She ran upstairs to her room to tidy her hair and wash her hands—and to brace herself to go downstairs to the kitchen again. She saw him disappearing into the bathroom as she left her room, and gave a sigh of relief.

CHAPTER SIX

No one was talkative over dinner. The two men exchanged a few remarks about the day's work, but Ellis thought Charlie was troubled about Leanne's absence. The meal was over quickly, and Ellis, alone in the kitchen, had dealt with the washing up and was giving some rather nervous attention to the two massive boxes of provisions when Steve came in. There were loaves and loaves of bread, several chickens, a great hunk of cheese, tins of sardines, more vegetables than she could get from the small vegetable garden in a month. How many shearers were there going to be? she was wondering worriedly, suddenly doubting that she would be able to manage after all.

It appeared, however, when she asked Steve, that there would be only four—plus the woolclasser, three shed hands, and Steve and Charlie. Ten men, she calculated mentally.

She asked shakily, 'What time will breakfast be?'

'Just listen,' said Steve. 'You needn't think up the questions, I'm going to tell you exactly what you have to do. To begin with, the men don't sleep here. They're local men and they come after they've breakfasted— and they go home for their dinner at night. Work starts at seven-thirty, and Charlie and I will be in the shed at that hour too. The men knock off at nine-thirty for half an hour for morning lunch and from three till three-thirty for afternoon lunch. You'll make sandwiches and tea for then. Midday dinner is twelve, and it won't always be mutton. You'll remember the men have hefty appetites—shearing is exhausting work. Can you cook a big hearty dinner for eight? We'll have our dinner at night with you.'

'Yes,' said Ellis, with a certainty she was far from feeling, and wished vainly that Leanne was there, if only to give her moral support.

'You've got those hours fixed firmly in your mind? They're fixed by the union and they're to be strictly adhered to. We'll take all this stuff over to the old homestead near the shearing shed. You'll use the kitchen there, there's plenty of equipment, but no dishwasher—you'll find you don't have a lot of spare time by the time you've done the washing up. The men knock off at five-thirty, and Charlie and I will be ready for dinner here at seven. Have you got all that in your head?'

'Yes,' she said stiffly.

'You can come along with me while I take these provisions over so you can get your bearings.'

'All right,' she agreed, unwilling to go out in the night with him but knowing there was logic in it.

The yards outside the big shearing shed were full of sheep, and the holding pens inside were full too. Ellis helped Steve take the foodstuffs into the kitchen of the old homestead, and she had a look at the big dining room that opened off it. That was where she'd be serving dinner—tomorrow.

As they drove back home, the night was pitch dark, the sky cloudy. Steve garaged the car and Ellis didn't wait for him but called goodnight and hurried ahead into the house and up to her room. She closed her door and thought nervously of the next day. It was going to put her boast of efficiency really to the test! She was just about to start undressing when Steve rapped at the door, and she went to open it quickly, knowing he'd only open it himself if she didn't.

'Yes?' she said, her voice cold.

He pushed past her and shut the door with his foot, and she felt her heart begin to beat treacherously fast.

'What do you want?' she demanded, by some miracle keeping her voice from shaking.

'I'm accepting the invitation you tossed me earlier on.'

'What—what invitation?'

'To come and get my ring.'

Stupefied, she watched him stride across to the dressing table and pick up the small red box. She saw the emerald flash as he opened it and took the ring out. 'I'd like you to wear it, Ellis,' he said, and now as he looked at her across the room it was his eyes that were flashing. 'Can't I—persuade you?'

She shook her head. 'Your particular form of persuasion doesn't work on me.'

His long mouth lifted at the corners. 'I thought it was beginning to,' he suggested. 'I thought you were beginning to discover you might even enjoy being my wife.'

'I'm sorry, but I wouldn't,' she said, and knew she sounded prim—which was, if she thought about it, laughable.

He put the ring down and came closer to her. 'What's Martin Webster been saying to you about me?' he asked intently.

'Nothing,' she stammered, and felt her cheeks crimson.

'Nothing?' he repeated, and suddenly he had a hand on either side of her jaw and was tilting her face to his.

'Just that you're a—cynic,' she said indistinctly. She saw his pupils dilate and then her glance went as though compelled to his mouth.

'You knew that,' he said. 'I told you so myself. Did he advise you not to marry me?'

'I—I didn't tell him you'd asked me.'

His expression was mocking. 'You cheeped out your little story about being my housekeeper, I suppose,' he taunted.

'Something like that,' she agreed. With a violent movement she pulled herself free of his hands and stood looking at him defiantly. 'But I'm certainly not going to stay here and cook for your shearers if you're going to pester me. I'll—I'll leave. I'll take the plane out tomorrow.'

He smiled crookedly. 'I believe you're threatening me, Ellis. It won't work, you know. You can walk out any time it pleases you—now, if you like. I'll manage. The shearers will be fed if I have to cook for them myself—I'm quite capable of doing it, make no mistake. Everything will go without a hitch, so don't try to fool yourself I can't get along without you.'

Ellis bit her lip. He really didn't care if she went. He had the most detestable knack of knowing how to decimate her belief in her usefulness. He'd never been in the least impressed by her capabilities, he'd never given her one word of praise for anything she'd done.

She stammered angrily, 'I'm not fooling myself. I'm quite sure you can get along without *anybody*, Steve Gascoyne!'

He raised his dark eyebrows. 'We're talking about you in particular. In your specific role as shearers' cook,' he added. 'But I don't want to be rid of Ellis Lincoln. I'm beginning to like having a pretty girl around the place ... So right, as from now I'll treat you as you wish. You'll go on the wages sheet as shearers' cook.' Ellis stared at him blankly, hardly able to take in what he was saying.

'That's what you want, isn't it?' he said mockingly. Then with a brusque, 'Goodnight,' he let himself out of the room.

Ellis's knees felt suddenly weak. He had gone, and he had promised to leave her alone. She had won her point.

She stared vacantly at the spot where only a moment ago he had stood, and she could still feel the intensity of his green gaze. She had won—yet, curiously, she didn't feel she had won at all. In some puzzling way, she knew that *he* had won, and she suspected he was well aware of it.

Steve kept his promise. For the next few days he left her alone—in the sense she had meant it, that was. But that didn't mean that everything went smoothly between them. It didn't.

Despite her belief in her own dependability, she made mistakes. She was late with afternoon lunch the very first day and he came angrily over to the old homestead where she was hastily loading the hamper of sandwiches and the huge pot of tea into the car.

'How much longer are you going to take, for God's sake? I told you the breaks the men take are rigid. They have half an hour exactly, and they don't expect to wait around for half of that time and then have to gulp their tucker.'

'I'm sorry.' Ellis's face was flushed. 'The—the clearing up after dinner took me longer than I expected——'

'Don't make excuses. The clearing up can wait, the men can't. Now get a move on. I'm paying you awarded wages, so keep on the ball, do you understand. Otherwise I'll sack you for incompetence.'

His words stung and Ellis didn't dare to glance at him. He could have no idea how it hurt her pride to be taken to task like this. Somehow she hadn't expected it of him. She almost wished she'd gone on the plane to-day—back to Uncle Bill. She had a strange feeling that she had grown stronger while she'd been away—that if she went back to Melbourne now it wouldn't really break her heart to see Jan and Paul together.

She got into the car, and failed to start it, and heard Steve mutter an oath.

'Get over,' he grated, and she moved across the seat feeling a mixture of anger and fear. He got the car go-ing with a jerk and a roar and neither of them spoke as he drove the couple of hundred yards to the shearing shed. Ellis felt a mass of nerves as she carried the ham-per up the steps. The men were already sitting near the table around the big wool bins, and she murmured an apology and withdrew quickly. They had all been very polite to her at dinner time. She had given them plenty to eat—she had cooked too much, actually—but she thought they'd enjoyed their meal.

Now she stood in the dust at the foot of the steps and looked absentmindedly at the sheep—the woolly ones waiting to be shorn, the strangely white ones that had emerged from the tally pens—and thought about the men in the shed. They'd have been a whole lot friend-lier and relaxed if she'd really looked like the cook, she was certain, or—or if she'd been Mrs Steve Gascoyne. As it was, they were uncertain of her. The wool classer, Mike, was the only one who'd said more than Good-day to her so far, and he'd asked where she was from—and then Steve had come along and he hadn't said any-thing more.

Over in the sunshine, Steve had the bonnet of the car up and was tinkering about with the engine, and Ellis stood uncertainly. She had an impulse to go back into the shed and watch the shearing. One of the dogs came bounding down the steps and brushed past her in a friendly frolicsome way. This morning, she'd seen him lying cosily in the wool in one of the sorting bins, but he'd been very quickly called to order.

Suddenly she felt really tired. She still had a lot to do—and then there'd be dinner to prepare for herself and the two Gascoynes. How much easier it would have been with Leanne here to help!

Presently Steve slammed down the bonnet of the car and came towards her. 'It should be all right now,' he said briefly, and went into the shearing shed. Ellis waited another ten minutes before she went inside to deal with the debris from afternoon lunch.

'You're doing a good job, Ellis,' Charlie told her next day. 'Why don't you come in and watch the shearing? You're quite welcome, you know.'

'Some time,' Ellis said with a smile. 'I'm in a bit of a rush right now—I have to get the dinner going.'

'It's a shame you have it all on your own,' he said apologetically. 'Leanne shouldn't have deserted. It's impossible to get a cook on this island—the women always turn to and do it, but it's hardly fair on you since you're a guest.'

She coloured and said with embarrassment, 'I'm on the payroll, you know. I'm not working for nothing.'

At exactly that point Steve came up the steps. 'You'd better get back in the shed,' he told his brother curtly, and Charlie melted away instantly. 'My brother's on the payroll too,' he told Ellis equally curtly. 'We've got four shearers and they shear mighty fast. No one has time to stand about listening to women chatter.'

Ellis clenched her teeth and kept silent, though she longed to make some stinging retort. Stupid, she told herself. Now he was treating her as the boss would treat the cook, why couldn't she be satisfied? What did she want from him? She stole a look at him and discovered he was rolling a cigarette and paying absolutely no attention to her. She might not have existed. *He* didn't think to ask her if she'd like to watch the shearing, she thought resentfully.

That day she made a delectable sauce to go with the roast chicken. The men polished it all off and she felt very pleased with herself. Steve had told her 'plain food,' but it just went to show they appreciated subtle seasonings. Gratified by her success, Ellis added date and walnut sandwiches to the cheese and sardine for afternoon lunch—and was chagrined later to discover they'd given her fancy stuff to their dogs. Worse still, Steve was there and fully aware of it. He told her, grabbing her by the arm harder than he had any right to do, 'No fancy stuff, Ellis. You're not catering for a tea-party.'

She swallowed. 'I'm sorry.'

'Being sorry's no use. Just follow orders.'

Ellis didn't look at him. She'd thought of staying in the shed awhile to watch, but changed her mind. She'd had one reprimand and she didn't want another. He'd accuse her of wasting time—distracting the shearers. Anything.

The rest of the week passed reasonably smoothly—except that Ellis was beginning to feel she could sleep for a week, and she was sick of the very sight of food —and of the washing up bowl! On Friday she managed to spend a little time in the shed. Steve had taken the jeep out and when the men resumed work at three-thirty she stood near the big wool bins where she hoped she wouldn't be in the way, interested to see what went on. It was fascinating to watch one of the shearers open the little gate into the catching pen, seize a sheep behind its front legs, then sit it on its hindquarters and drag it over to the shearing stand where the electric clippers hung. A few expert strokes, and the belly was trimmed, then with long sweeps the fleece was removed from each side of the body. After that it seemed no time at all till the sheep was being pushed through the trapdoor that led into the tally pen below. There was not a moment wasted, and wouldn't want to be—because a good shearer could shear a hundred and fifty sheep a day! The dogs were enjoying themselves enormously, and when more sheep had to be let through to the catching pens, they would race over the sheep's backs and urge them to go where they were wanted.

Most intriguing of all, however, was to watch one of the hands pick up the newly shorn fleece and throw it on to the big classing table, where it came down all in one piece and looking absolutely enormous. There the dirty wool was removed, the fleece was classed, then rolled deftly into a bundle and tossed into one of the sorting bins.

Ellis watched for quite a while before she reluctantly moved away to take up her own tasks again.

Saturday the shearers didn't work, and it was bliss to have an easy day. Ellis didn't even get up for breakfast—Steve had told her not to. 'You look really whacked, Ellis,' he'd said, though he hadn't sounded in the least sympathetic. 'Your weekends are free, you know.'

Ellis could have wept her relief, but shearers' cooks don't weep.

It was Charlie who called her down to lunch on Saturday. She'd slept till all hours—she hadn't the faintest interest in breakfast and no one had offered her even a cup of tea or coffee—then she'd taken a long leisurely shower and washed her hair. She felt reasonably happy with her week's work, and yet at the same time she felt vaguely dissatisfied. Was it because Steve hadn't once said, 'You've done a good job'? He'd been so relentlessly hard on her all the week, as if she were no more than she had insisted she was—the cook.

She was dressed and her golden-brown hair was brushed out and shining when Charlie called at her door, 'Are you coming down, Ellis? Lunch is ready.'

Someone, she discovered, had prepared a delicious salad—built around avocado halves filled with a creamed crab mixture—the sort of thing you'd expect from a quality restaurant.

'It's crayfish, not crab,' Steve said when she commented on it. 'Local crays—and I bought the avocados the other day in Whitemark. You like it, do you?'

'It's fabulous,' she said after a second. It cost her an effort to admit it, because he must have prepared it, and it was a little deflating to find he really could cook.

She saw his mouth curve sardonically. 'Thanks for your generous praise.'

Ellis flushed and looked away from him. He and Charlie talked about shearing. One of the shearers was slow, and Steve remarked that he wouldn't employ him next year if he didn't smarten himself up. Ellis thought it unfair but didn't say so—she knew the men were paid according to the number of sheep they sheared.

'You're looking disapproving, Ellis,' said Steve. 'I'm not penalising the guy for being slow, but for doing a crook job in his determination to equal the others in numbers. He should satisfy himself with less money till he becomes more expert.'

Ellis felt crushed, but she wasn't going to apologise —after all, she hadn't said a word!

Presently Charlie remarked, 'I had a letter from

Leanne yesterday. She's planning a few days at Koolong.'

'I wish her joy of it,' said Steve, and a rather awkward silence fell. Ellis broke it by asking brightly, 'Are you going to North East River this weekend, Charlie? If you are, I'd like to go with you. I saw Martin Webster in town one day, and I promised to come if you were going.'

'Is that so?' Charlie sounded uneasy but not oversurprised—and Ellis knew Leanne must have told him she was the Websters' cousin. 'Well, I did think of going fishing tomorrow, so——'

'You'll have to go alone,' Steve cut in gratingly. 'Ellis is coming for a picnic to the beach with me.'

Ellis felt a curious sense of shock. This was the first she'd heard of a beach picnic—and she wasn't going. Yet though she opened her mouth to say so, she kept quiet after all. 'Not in front of Charlie,' she told herself uneasily. Then afterwards, when she went into the kitchen to help with the washing up, Steve said, 'Keep out, Ellis. This is your free day, remember.'

'What about tomorrow?' she flared. 'Isn't that free too? I didn't say I'd go picnicking with you. I want to go to North East River.'

'And I happen to want to take you to the beach,' he retorted.

She stared at him and felt her resolve weaken. She felt herself drowning in the green of his eyes—and that was positively not permissible.

'Is it union rules I should do what you say?' she heard herself ask ridiculously, and he gave her a brief laugh.

'In this case—yes.'

She didn't see either Steve or Charlie the rest of the day. For want of something better to do, she went into

the kitchen and did some baking. She made a cake that
was a favourite with Uncle Bill—a very unusual cake
that contained, incredible though it sounded, a tin of
tomato soup and half a glass of sherry. She iced it with
cream cheese and decorated it with cherries, then wondered what in heaven's name she was going to do with
it. She could not in a million years serve it up to the
shearers! She knew what they'd do with it! Incon-
sequentially, she thought of Leanne, at Koolong now,
no doubt, and probably enjoying the social life, and
the freedom from work. How bored she'd have been
this week at Warrianda! But Ellis hadn't been bored—
she'd been far too busy.

It wasn't till some hours later, when she'd eaten
alone in the empty house, that she began to feel a little
neglected, and determinedly she found her writing pad
and began to write to Jake.

She wrote a whole two pages—her hand simply ran
away with her—and then discovered she was listening.
For what? For them to come home. For—for that mad-
dening, incomprehensible man Steve Gascoyne to come
home. Deep in her heart, however she tried to hide the
knowledge from herself, she knew that she longed to
have him knock at her door, burst in on her, say outrageous things, infuriate her.

Take her in his arms.

Ellis forced herself back to her letter . . .

On Sunday, she discovered that Steve's statement
that he was taking her to the beach was no empty
threat, and that she hadn't a hope of getting her own
way. She was upstairs making her bed when he came
into the room and she straightened up and looked at
him, feeling a wave of colour sweep over her face.

'When you've finished in here, Ellis,' he told her
coolly, 'you can go downstairs and get a picnic to-

gether. I'll be ready to leave when you are.'

His eyes challenged her, but somehow she didn't feel like indulging in an argument with him in the bedroom, so she said a weak and reluctant, 'Very well,' and turned her back on him. She told herself she'd get the picnic together, but she wouldn't go out with him. She was going to North East River with Charlie.

In the kitchen, she had packed up cold meat, salad vegetables, and bread and butter, and was filling a thermos with tea when he appeared and asked her, 'Right?'

'Yes. Your picnic's ready,' she said agreeably, 'but I'm not coming with you. I'm going with Charlie. I want to see Martin.'

'Then that's too bad,' he drawled. 'Charlie left half an hour ago. You'll have to make do with me.'

Ellis felt a pulse begin to beat in her temples. She felt really enraged, and half her anger was directed at Charlie. He knew she wanted to go with him, yet he'd driven off without checking whether she was coming or not. Leanne was right—he did whatever Steve wanted, regardless of her or of his wife or of anyone. She said heatedly, 'I won't have to make do with you, Mr Gascoyne. I don't need to go anywhere. I can entertain myself here perfectly well—like I did yesterday. Besides, you—you promised you wouldn't pester me,' she finished uncertainly.

'Oh, I'm not forgetting you're the shearers' cook,' he said ironically. 'But a picnic with the boss is just one of the perks the cook can expect on weekends—if she's fetching enough. I'll leave you alone, but I don't fancy going out by myself. I used to take my aunt for a drive to the beach on Sundays,' he added after a brief pause. He sounded suddenly sombre. 'She liked to sit in the car knitting or doing crossword puzzles while I took a swim.'

Ellis looked at him suspiciously through her lashes. There was a hint of softness on his face that she'd never seen before and she turned away from it quickly, unwilling to admit to herself that he might be human after all. He caught her by the arm.

'You'd better come, Ellis,' he said briefly. 'Get your swimmers and I'll see you out at the car. And don't worry—we'll stick to a basic boss–employee relationship, if that's the way you want it.'

She grimaced at his back as he went through the door. It looked as if she had to go, she told herself. And anyhow, she would enjoy a swim—and she didn't fancy another day on her own. She'd take her one-piece costume, though—not her bikini.

She had the picnic basket all ready, then at the last minute she got down the cake tin. She'd take the cake she'd baked yesterday. Why not? She pictured Steve being just a little bit intrigued by the soft warm colour and the subtle flavouring. Yet why should she care if he was intrigued or not? she asked herself crossly.

The beach he took her to was not the one she had been to before, but it was just as empty. There was not a soul in sight, and she didn't move as Steve prepared to get out of the car.

'What's the matter?' he asked, raising one eyebrow.

She licked her top lip nervously. 'It's—it's so deserted.'

'What's wrong with that? Don't I remember you saying you liked quiet places—that night you told me about your fiancé on Flinders? Remember?'

Of course she remembered, and she felt mortified.

'At all events,' he went on reasonably, 'most of the beaches round here are unfrequented. That's why I brought you along with me—to make sure I had some company.'

Ellis said no more. She climbed out of the car, then stood looking about her for a moment. It was all so beautiful—white, white sands, great rocks covered in red and yellow and orange lichen, water like the palest aquamarine. The rocks glittered like jewels in the sun and presently she discovered there were great prisms of quartz in them that reflected the sun's light. Back from the curve of the beach there were tea-tree groves and dark pines, and the granite mountains made a magnificent backdrop.

Steve took the picnic basket, and a few minutes later, in the shelter of a group of huge rounded rocks, Ellis changed into her swimsuit. It was black and backless, with narrow straps and a deeply plunging neckline. Its simplicity was broken only by a scattering of eyelets of varying sizes arranged to form a pattern from the V across her diaphragm and stomach and finishing above her left thigh. Her skin showed whitely against the black, and she looked up at the blueness of the sunny sky. She tanned quickly and comfortably when she had a chance, and by the end of today she'd have lost that unsunned look.

Steve was in very brief Vandyke brown trunks, and Ellis caught her breath. He wasn't looking in her direction and she studied him swiftly. His body was muscular and bronzed, his shoulders broad, his hips narrow, and he looked dark against the white of the sand and the clear pallor of the languorous sea. He turned and saw her at last, his eyes skimming over her figure. She didn't feel self-conscious in this cover-up, but the memory of last time they had been on the beach together sent the colour surging into her face.

'Are you coming into the water?' he asked rather

tersely. 'Or are you one of those water sprites who's strictly ornamental?'

For answer, Ellis ran past him into the sea, and did a quick porpoise dive.

CHAPTER SEVEN

THEY stayed in the water till they were both growing hungry, then came out to eat. Steve had brought a portable ice box that held a few cans of beer and lemonade, and they kept the thermos for later by mutual consent. At the end of the meal, Ellis produced the tin containing her cake, and he watched her take the lid off, then commented, 'Looks like a birthday cake. Don't tell me you're twenty-one today.'

'No, it's nothing special,' she said, feeling a little foolish.

'I don't eat cake,' he said as she cut into it, and she paused, feeling a sense of fury, till he added nonchalantly, 'Still, I'll try it.'

By then she didn't much care what his comment was. He'd spoiled her little moment of triumph, yet what had she expected?

'Nice,' he said, when he'd bitten into the slice she handed him.

'Thank you,' she said coldly.

'But no good for the shearers,' he commented next. 'They'd probably give it to their dogs.'

'You—you don't know how to pay a compliment, do you?' she stuttered, and he looked at her in mocking surprise.

'In my recollection, shearers' cooks aren't particularly interested in comments—they're only interested in their pay cheques.'

Ellis, who had a sweet tooth and had been looking forward to her slice of cake, put it down almost untouched, her enthusiasm gone. She longed to tell him he was boorish, but instead she choked out, 'I don't wonder Leanne can't live with you.'

He raised his eyebrows. 'What do you mean by that?'

'You're—you're inhuman! You don't care for anyone's feelings.'

'What in God's name are we discussing?' he asked. 'I thought we were talking about pay cheques—and cake.'

'*My* cake,' she retorted, and he looked at her, his green eyes cool. She could feel her breast heaving and was annoyed with herself for getting so worked up about nothing.

'Women always want to bring personalities into a conversation,' he remarked, and leaned forward to cut another slice of cake.

'I'm not bringing personalities into anything,' she said furiously.

'You mentioned Leanne.'

'Yes,' she snapped, completely losing all sense of logic. 'And I don't blame her for wanting to get out of Warrianda. If she has any sense she—she'll never come back!'

Steve finished his cake without a word, then stretched out on his back on the sand, his hands behind his head. Ellis cast him one look, then began to cram everything back into the basket.

'If we're talking about Leanne,' he said lazily after a moment, looking at her from between his half-shut lids, 'then it's my opinion a woman should be prepared to go where her man goes. That way, he can be reasonably sure she loves him as much as what he stands for. If Leanne won't stick to Charlie here, you're right. He might as well be rid of her.'

'Charlie mightn't agree with you about that,' she retorted. She was trying to calm down and, to tell the truth, she didn't know why she had this desire to quarrel with him, but she had. She was feeling very antagonistic, and the way he lay there, supine, indolent, maddened her. 'While she's here,' she continued, 'Leanne has only half of him.'

Steve turned his head towards her sharply, his eyes glinting green between lids half closed against the sun. The dark hair on his chest glistened, and she turned her eyes away from it and knew he was watching her as he said lazily, 'Now what the hell do you mean by *that*?'

'He—he's loyal to you, not to her,' she said quickly. 'He does what *you* want, not what she wants. He—he listens to *you* all the time.' She was sitting back on her heels, her hands clasped together on her thighs, and she could see them trembling as he kept his head turned slightly and watched her.

'Look, I don't want to quarrel with you about other people's marital problems,' he said, suddenly rolling over on to his stomach and propping his chin on one hand. 'But you really ought to do a little straight thinking, Ellis, if Charlie and Leanne are on your mind. My brother's learning how to manage sheep while he's here with me, and in my opinion if you make your money out of wool then that's a wise thing to do. I made an offer to take him on and he took it up of his own free will. Colin wasn't keen to have him at Koolong—he'd been there after he left school, then he decided sheep farming wasn't for him and he got out and did nothing in particular in Melbourne. That's why Colin won't be bothered with him. But Charlie's at liberty to get his know-how wherever he can. How you connect his choosing Warrianda with lack of loyalty to his wife I just don't know.'

'You're—you're not helping their marriage,' she said after a moment. It was the first she had heard of Charlie's background, and though she was half convinced by what Steve had told her, she didn't want to be.

'Leanne's not helping the marriage,' he retorted. He lowered his head and rested his cheek on his forearm. 'You women are all the same—threatening to walk out if you don't get your own way. Your cousin Jan walked out on me because she thought I'd fly up to Melbourne and beg her to come back to me, and promise we'd live wherever she wanted, which wasn't here. Leanne's trying the same tactics on Charlie—and it remains to be seen what success she has. I hope none. No man who values his self-respect can allow a woman to run him—she has her territory, he has his—and it's bad news when one of them gets greedy and tries to take over.' He stopped, and Ellis found her thoughts were back with what he'd said about Jan. That had really jolted her. Jan hadn't broken with Steve because she'd fallen madly in love with Paul after all. She'd sent back her ring imagining Steve would give in, allow her to have what she wanted—and that was Koolong, of course. Martin had said so. Was Jan regretting her hastiness now? Ellis wondered. Certainly she wasn't yet engaged to Paul——

She felt a shock of surprise when Steve sat up and looked at her quizzically and remarked, 'And then there's Ellis, of course. But you're the one who *did* get her own way, aren't you, my little moonbird?'

Her eyes fell from his. She drew a circle on the sand. 'I—I don't know what you mean.'

'Oh, surely you do! You threatened to walk out on

me, didn't you? And I gave in. I installed you as shearers' cook—you're having it all just the way you want it. Are you satisfied?'

She stared at him, her pale face suffusing with colour. Something in the way he was looking at her unnerved her completely.

'Well, are you?' he repeated.

She didn't answer, but bit her lip and looked down at the sand. Unexpectedly, he reached out and knocked her off balance. There was a brief struggle and then she was lying against him on the sand. One arm held her pinioned to him and she could feel his bare thighs against her own. She pulled her head back and tried to jerk herself free of him, but it was a futile effort. His eyes were looking into hers and she could see the salt on his thick dark lashes, drawing them into points. There were tiny flecks of gold in the green of his eyes and she gazed and gazed, feeling herself being submerged.

Submerged in every way. A feeling of sensual warmth was spreading right through her, from her lips to her thighs. She knew she hadn't been satisfied when she got what she wanted. She'd hated it. And at this moment she realised it to the full. This was what she wanted—to be here, held against him intimately, in a place that was so secluded it seemed no one else existed. His thighs were against hers and his flat muscular belly pressed against her own, and his eyes looked deeply into hers. His lips were curving sensually now, as if they were on the point of taking her own. Ellis hungered for the touch of his lips—she'd forgotten what his kiss was like. She could feel her heart pounding and she was aware that one of her shoulder straps had slipped and that the V of her neckline had widened to reveal more of her breast than was decent, but she didn't care.

Steve's mouth covered hers briefly, passionately, then moved to her shoulder and she felt the warmth of his lips, and the hardness of his teeth against her flesh. She was melting—she was slipping into an ecstatic oblivion—when suddenly she thought of Jan, and pushed against him with all her strength.

He sat up abruptly, away from her, and she turned her own tormented body in against the sand, closing her eyes and moaning silently. She hated herself for wanting to be in his arms. She meant absolutely nothing to him—she was just another woman.

'Don't tell me I've broken my promise,' he said, his voice uneven. 'You knew this would happen when you came, didn't you?' She felt his arm come across her back and his fingers dig into her upper arm as he tried to pull her over to face him, but she resisted, pressing her face and her bosom into the warm dry sand.

'Come on, Ellis—come back to me. Isn't it what you want?'

'No,' she said, and added violently, 'Don't touch me!'

His hand was withdrawn and when he spoke again his voice was frigidly accusing.

'Does this sort of thing amuse you, then, you cruel little bitch?'

She flinched at his tone. He certainly knew how to turn everything inside out, and it confused her utterly. He was blaming her for this now, when his was the impulse that had started it, his the force that had brought her into his arms.

'Not as much as it amuses you,' she said, her voice low. 'You—you have a low opinion of women, haven't you, Steve Gascoyne?'

'Perhaps,' he said.

'Of me,' she insisted. She sat up, but felt unable just now to look him in the eye.

'Don't take it that way—don't let's make it personal,' he said roughly. 'I'm not using you as an object to relieve my carnal appetite, if that's what your hinting at, Ellis. I know I've acted like a savage, but you're at least half to blame. I've offered you a ring, haven't I? And asked you not once but several times to marry me. God knows I don't like this relationship of boss–employee you seem intent on inflicting on us. I don't get what I need out of having you mess around baking cakes for me, either. It's in my bed I want you, not in my kitchen.'

'You wanted Jan in your bed,' she accused, and as she said it she reflected that he'd probably had Jan in his bed anyhow. 'You—you asked *her* to marry you——you can—you can still have her. She and Paul aren't engaged—Martin told me so the other day.'

There was silence for several seconds, then she turned her head and saw Steve was looking at her with eyes that smouldered speculatively.

'So that's what you were finding out in Whitemark the other day, is it? Well, it's great news. All our tears in vain—yours and mine. But if you're making plans for me, don't bother. I won't be stepping down. I'm not built that way—it goes against the grain, as you should know by now.' He got up and stood towering over her, tall and broad and masculine. 'Well, are you coming in for another swim? I know *I* need to cool off.'

Ellis lowered her head. She felt bruised, hurt, through all her physical being. She didn't know how he could talk about swimming, cooling off, when he must know she was in a turmoil with everything up in the air—unresolved.

Her voice trembling, she told him, 'I'm going to sunbathe.'

'All right.'

She watched him stride away, then plunge into the unbearably beautiful sea, and she lay down and pressed her cheek against the sand and felt tears squeeze between her lids. How hopeless and idiotic to fall in love with a man who had no real feelings!

Because that was exactly what she had done . . .

She sunbathed and dozed uneasily for the remainder of the afternoon, and it was only with an effort that she stirred herself when Steve came and flicked water on her and told her roughly, 'Come on—up! Get dressed and we'll be on our way.'

She rolled on to her side and lay staring at him, more than half expecting him to reach down and pull her to her feet—and into his arms. But he simply stood, hands on his lean hips, looking down at her enigmatically.

'What's the matter? Do you want a helping hand?' he asked, his eyes glinting.

So he was waiting for her to make the first gesture —and if she did, and if she landed in his arms, it would be at least half her fault. And if she pulled away he'd call her a cruel little bitch.

'If you're waiting for me to manhandle you,' he said with a sort of controlled savageness, 'you're waiting in vain. I'm sorely tempted to force you to surrender to me, but I'm not going to do it. When shearing's over —and you're committed to me till then, don't forget—we'll take stock, and you can disappear back to Melbourne. If that's what you want.'

Her heart thudded. It wasn't what she wanted—not remotely. But it was what she'd have to do. She couldn't accept him on his terms, without love.

She scrambled to her feet with a sudden movement and ran down to the sea. The water was cold against her languid sun-warmed body, the sun was going down, and though she struck out and swam vigorously, she soon began to shiver and to feel icy right through to her bones. In her heart she longed to have Steve come into the water to get her. She wanted him to hold her close in the salty sea, to taste his lips warm and sweet on her mouth. She wanted the slipperiness of his wet body against hers—she wanted him to say he loved her. She wanted to—to die in his arms.

She swallowed on a sob. The terrible thing was that he didn't even believe in love—and he saw marriage as a game of makebelieve, nothing more.

She managed to regain control of herself at last, but she was still cold as she left the water, blinking the salt and the tears from her eyes, and feeling her hair cling stickily to her head. The white beach was empty and for a mad moment she thought he'd driven off and left her. But the car was still in the shade of the trees.

She found her clothes behind the rocks where she had left them and peeled her sodden swimsuit from her shivering body, then rubbed herself dry with her towel. It wasn't a beach towel, it was one she'd brought from the homestead, and it was soft and delicately plushy on one side, rough and stimulating on the other. She dried herself on the rough side, then draped it round her shoulders, velvet side against her skin, while she pulled on her panties and her white cotton jeans. She'd picked up her bra when she heard Steve coming, and in a panic she pulled her shirt over her head, wrapped her bra in the towel, then stepped out from the shelter of the rocks, to find herself caught in a cool evening wind that blew straight in off the sea, and set her shivering again.

Steve was waiting for her.

'Come on, come on,' he said testily, and she snapped back,

'What's the hurry? Have you got a date? Or—or can't you wait to get rid of me?'

His eyes raked over her and she felt her nipples harden with cold, so that they pressed against her clinging shirt.

'Unless you're intent on being provocative,' he said, his eyes obviously missing nothing, 'you should have put on your bra.'

She didn't answer, but she burned with shame and anger.

The minute they reached home, she ran upstairs to her room. She wished she could disappear tomorrow, but she couldn't. She'd agreed to look after the shearers, and she'd do it. She wondered wretchedly how she and Steve could possibly resume their boss–employee relationship after today. But with Steve, as she had already learned, anything was possible. It was different for him, anyhow. His emotions weren't involved. While he might be caught up by his passions once in a while, they were purely physical. They left no painful aftermath of unsated hungry emotions such as she was experiencing now; that was plain.

When she went downstairs the meal was ready and the table laid. Charlie had caught several flounder which he'd cooked, and he had opened a bottle of white wine. Ellis accepted a glass as she sat down at the table.

'Did you see Martin, Charlie?' she asked brightly as they started on their dinner. The lights were low and for this she was thankful as she had the nervy feeling that the events of the afternoon were written on her face like a musical score, and she didn't know who she wanted to hide it from most—Charlie or Steve.

'Sure I saw him,' said Charlie, helping himself to salad. 'He was disappointed you didn't come.'

'What did you tell him?' she asked after a second.

'I said Steve had taken you swimming. He seemed to have the idea you were working here.' He grimaced suddenly and added ruefully, 'I suppose you are too— like a trojan! Leanne told me Martin's your cousin.'

'Yes. I've lived with the Websters since I was about fourteen. My parents died in a boating accident when I was eleven, and my father's best friend, Jake Armour, and his wife more or less adopted me.'

She saw Steve's lashes flick up in surprise.

'Jake Armour?' he repeated.

'Yes,' she said, her colour high. 'Don't you remember he was at the hotel in Hobart?' He said nothing and she resumed her story mainly out of nervousness. 'Jake went broke—he used to gamble, I suppose—so he and Siddie couldn't go on looking after me, and I went to the Websters. Funnily enough, only a few years later Siddie and Jake came into a lot of money, though Siddie didn't live to enjoy it very long. They wanted me to come back to them, but I really couldn't leave my aunt. She wasn't well, and Jan was——' She stopped on the point of saying that Jan was helpless in the house and changed it to, 'Jan was doing an art course at the tech. I'd just left school and started in the bank, but it didn't matter—it wasn't as if I had a career ahead of me.'

'Then your aunt died,' Steve said thoughtfully.

'Yes. So you see I was really needed. It wouldn't have been fair to walk out when they'd been so good to me. Anyhow, I was happy—I had friends.'

She saw Steve's mouth twist cynically and supposed he was thinking of Paul, who had turned out to be not such a good friend after all, and she set her lips and turned to Charlie. 'Did Martin have any—special news from home?'

'No, I don't think so. He said to tell you he'll be leaving Flinders soon and hopes to see you in the meantime.'

Ellis nodded. She thought Charlie was very tactful to say nothing about Jan, and she supposed the whole set-up must be rather a mystery to him. She had the feeling he knew better than to be inquisitive about Steve's affairs, and she was quite sure Steve wouldn't give away much about his personal life.

The conversation presently returned to the shearing, and Steve remarked that, provided it didn't rain, it should be finished by the end of the week. Ellis stopped listening. As soon as that? And then—Steve had as good as said she could go. He—he wasn't going to force her to surrender.

She thought about the situation later as she sat at her mirror, brushing her hair. Some part of her longed to tell Steve that she didn't want to go—she'd be happy living here for ever—she'd marry him. But he didn't love her. No way could she fool herself that he did. And she couldn't—*couldn't* marry a man who didn't love her. He'd asked Jan first, and that made asking *her* almost a humiliation. She meant absolutely nothing to him. Again and again she was brought up against that thought and it was like running into a brick wall. She couldn't alter the facts, she couldn't pretend he had seen her and fallen in love with her. One girl was as good as another—except that she was very well aware that Jan's attractions outweighed her own by a ton. And she couldn't help thinking it was quite on the cards that Jan would eventually give in when she found Steve wouldn't. Despite his hardness, he was a powerfully attractive man.

Ellis prayed that this week he would continue to treat her as the cook and nothing else. She didn't want him to be tempted again to force her to surrender, because he might succeed.

In the morning, he wasn't at breakfast, and Charlie said he'd gone to Whitemark to pick up more provisions for the men. There was enough bread in the freezer for morning lunch, and Ellis was trying to start up the old bomb when his car came up the drive.

He got out of his car and watched her futile efforts for a moment, then came across to her.

'Move over,' he said briefly. 'There's a knack in starting this thing. I'll show you.'

Ellis moved over and though she watched while he demonstrated, she didn't really take in what he was telling her. She found she was too disturbed by his nearness. Finally he left the motor running and turned towards her, his eyes probing.

'Why didn't you tell me about Jake Armour before?' he asked unexpectedly.

She shrugged. 'What was the point? I told you from the start he was an old family friend and you made fun of that.'

'Because of what I'd seen with my own eyes. Any man would think what I did when he saw a girl like you accepting lavish gifts from an older and decidedly susceptible male. I still think he's in love with you, and you can't have forgotten you told me you didn't want to—live with him.'

'As his daughter,' she told him with a little spurt of anger. 'He's marrying again, if you want to know, and I'd be in the way. You have a—a foul mind!'

'All men who are men have foul minds,' he said imperturbably, 'so I won't pretend I haven't. What have you written home about me, by the way? Have you been making Paul jealous?'

Ellis flinched. 'I—I haven't written home at all,' she said jerkily.

His eyebrows rose. 'But you're making sure something gets back—via Martin Webster. Is that it?'

'No, it's not,' she retorted. 'And now would you please let me go—or morning lunch will be late and you'll be attacking me for—for breaking union rules.'

Steve got out of the car and slammed the door shut. 'I'll see you in the shed.'

If anything he was more impersonal than ever that week. Ellis worked hard and well, and seeing the mob of unshorn sheep diminishing, and the great bales of wool being loaded on to trucks from the landing platform in the shed, she became acutely aware that shearing was near completion. Steve had said no more to her about going back to Melbourne after the cut out. They would 'take stock' later, she supposed, and she lay awake at night, exhausted though she was, debating with herself as to what she was going to do, and unable to come to any real conclusion.

Charlie heard from Leanne during the week, but she didn't say when she would be back.

'I suppose you'll see about getting a housekeeper after the cut out,' she heard him ask Steve one night as she brought in the coffee at the end of the meal.

Steve glanced at her as he answered, his eyes enigmatic. 'I'm making no plans to go to Tasmania at the moment. I have other more pressing things to see to right here.' Ellis felt herself colouring, then felt a fool as he added, 'I want to get those wethers we've tagged cut out and trucked to Lady Barron ... Now if you'll both excuse me, I'm going to do some telephoning. We might as well celebrate the cut out, if nothing else.'

He took his coffee and disappeared, and Charlie said

with a frown, 'Steve's in a bad mood—something's bugging him.'

I am, Ellis thought, but she asked him, 'What did he mean about celebrating?'

'Oh, we have a bit of a do when shearing cuts out—the men like it and it's an excuse for everyone who wants to to get together and have a good time and exchange news and gossip. The word soon gets around —I wouldn't be surprised if your cousin Martin turns up.'

Ellis hoped he would. She badly wanted to know what was happening in Melbourne, and whether or not Jan and Paul were engaged. But it wasn't because she cared in the slightest about Paul. She had recovered from him with a completeness and a painlessness that was positively stupefying. It was only that—if there were no engagement, she'd begin to wonder if Jan would come back to Flinders...

The last sheep was shorn by five o'clock on Friday.

Steve had gone in to Whitemark after midday, returning with a couple of kegs of beer, lashings of bread, butter, and cheese, and a box full of salad vegetables. Charlie had killed a sheep on Wednesday and cut up half of it in the meathouse on Friday morning, so everything was well under way.

'You needn't concern yourself with this party, Ellis,' Steve told her as he dumped everything in the kitchen of the old homestead. 'It's not going to be your sort of entertainment—there'll probably only be one or two women along, and I doubt if anyone will be convinced you're part of the shearing team.'

Ellis flushed. 'I'd still like to have a look. Is Martin coming?'

'I wouldn't know. Why? Do you particularly want to see him?'

'Yes,' she said briefly. They looked at each other, then Ellis turned away. She was cleaning up for the last time. There were no more meals to prepare for the shearers. She felt a great mindless longing deep inside her. Steve hadn't touched her all the week, they had scarcely exchanged a word, he'd never come to her room——

'What's the attraction?' Steve asked, and she pulled herself up sharply and said quickly, 'I want to hear news from home, that's all.'

'You might let me hear what it is too,' he said dryly, 'seeing I'm an interested party.'

What that meant she was not quite sure, and she didn't ask.

The celebration was to be held in the shearing shed, and when her work was finished Ellis went back to the main homestead where she showered and then lay down on her bed to rest for a few minutes before she dressed. There was nothing for her to do tonight, no dinner to prepare. Steve and Charlie would be eating barbecued lamb over at the shearing shed, and so would she, and she hoped that Martin would be there too. Crazily, she longed to hear that Jan and Paul had announced their engagement. If someone had told her just a few weeks ago that she would welcome such news, she would never have believed it.

She fell asleep in the midst of her thoughts and when she woke a great golden moon had risen in a sky that had darkened to indigo. It looked so romantic and lovely floating above the trees that she could see from her bedroom window that her heart ached, and for a while she lay full of longing and confusion, aware that she had been dreaming of Steve and his kisses. Was he waiting for her to tell him she was leaving now the shearing was over? She didn't think he really cared whether she stayed or went; one woman was the same as another to him, so long as she did things his way. If Jan came back—if Jan gave in—that would satisfy him. He'd have a woman in his bed. He wouldn't miss Ellis. He didn't care for anyone.

Slipping her feet to the floor, she smiled wryly to herself. Anyone aware of her thoughts would think she disliked the man. Yet the very thought of him was enough to make her blood run quicker, and all sorts of unutterable desires flood her being.

She dressed in black pants and a silky black top with long sleeves that came in to a cuff. Ordinarily, she'd have worn something to dress it up, but on this occasion she decided it was better to forget about jewellery, and to look inconspicuous. As she left her room she felt decidedly nervous. There were going to be a lot of people in the shearing shed—a lot of men. What were they going to think about her? This was where it would have made all the difference in the world to be Steve's wife, or even his fiancée, and for a moment she was tempted to go back and slip the emerald ring on to her finger. Yet she couldn't make herself do it.

Oh damn, she thought despairingly. People would have to think what they liked. She had to see Martin —she only hoped he would be there.

CHAPTER EIGHT

OUTSIDE, she found she couldn't start the motor of the old car. Nothing would get the thing going. She didn't wonder that Leanne complained, and she couldn't think why Steve didn't provide her with something more roadworthy. It was all very well to criticise Leanne for not wanting to live at Warrianda, but he didn't do much to make it more attractive.

At last, since Charlie and Steve had been over at the shed for hours and it was obvious no one was coming back for her, she decided to walk. It was a good two kilometres and already it was dark. She found a torch and tried not to think about snakes. Steve had killed a tiger snake in the garden only a couple of nights ago, and she had often seen one—a tiger or a whipsnake or a copperhead—wriggling across the road when she was in the car. The track shone white in the moonlight, but the darkness of the scrub on either side worried her. She wasn't afraid of being molested—Mike, the wool-classer, had said there wasn't a safer place in the world than Flinders as far as people were concerned. Mothers could feel quite comfortable in their minds about their children, wherever they went on the island.

'But there's someone I'm afraid of,' Ellis thought as she walked steadily on along the road. While Steve Gascoyne was about, she didn't feel safe ...

The shearing shed was ablaze with lights. They'd be quite a tax on the generator, she caught herself thinking. She could smell the wool, and she could see the truck loaded with the last bales standing outside the loading platform. It was an ordeal to walk up the steps alone and into the shearing shed, and the unshaded lights dazzled her for a moment. There was a savoury smell of barbecued meat and, mingled with that, cigarette smoke and beer. The shed was full of men—she could see only a very few women, all of them older than she was, all of them looking very much at home amongst these tough country men. Ellis, unnoticed, shrank back in the shadows beyond the sorting bins, and wished she'd stayed at home. Behind the shearing stands a barbecue had been set up and Steve, looking very genial, was presiding over it. He hadn't seen her and she didn't want him to. The slatted classing table had been covered with a red and white checked cloth and two efficient-looking women were busily buttering slices of bread and piling them up on a huge china carving dish that she recognised as coming from the old homestead. Big brawny-looking men stood about drinking beer from glass mugs and talking volubly, while a few children, probably the shearers', scampered about drinking Coke and playing with the dogs.

Someone took Ellis by the arm and she jumped.

It was Martin—and she exclaimed in relief, 'Oh, Martin! How marvellous to see you! I was so hoping you'd be here—it's the only reason I came.'

'Ellis!' He was looking at her oddly. 'You're as white as a ghost! Have you been working too hard?'

Ellis couldn't tell him she'd lost her heart to a heartless man—and done what he'd warned her not to do, and she told him laughingly, 'Of course not. It's just that the damned car they let me use wouldn't work, and I had to walk over from the homestead. And I'm hungry. I've had nothing to eat—since breakfast,' she finished, remembering.

'Let me get you something,' he said at once. 'Come

along—they're nice people even if they do look rough, you don't have to feel shy.'

Ellis braced herself, but with Martin as an escort, everything was different. She didn't mind in the least if it was assumed she was his girl-friend, and of course it was. Jokes were made, suggestive questions asked as they made their way through the crowd and he introduced her to men he knew, and when he would have explained that she was his cousin, she pressed his arm and murmured, 'Don't worry, Martin—I don't mind.' Secretly, she was relieved. It explained her presence here if explanations were needed.

When they reached the barbecue, Steve frowned as she held out the plate she'd collected.

'You've taken your time coming. I thought you'd heeded my warning and decided to stay home.'

'I wanted to see Martin,' she retorted. 'But I couldn't get the car to start, and I had to walk.'

He picked up a juicy-looking chop between tongs and put it on her plate. 'I'd have been over in half an hour to check up on you.' He dished out some meat for Martin, then turned away to speak to someone else, and Ellis and Martin moved away to get some bread and butter.

'I get the idea Steve Gascoyne can't stand the sight of me,' Martin remarked cheerfully. 'Must be something to do with Jan. That girl must be off her brain to have returned his ring. As a matter of fact, she's pretty obviously having second thoughts.'

Ellis's heart lurched alarmingly, but right then she had to smile at the women presiding over the piles of bread and butter and listen with half an ear to some remark about Martin being a lucky young man. Word seemed to have got around pretty quickly that she belonged to Martin.

It wasn't till a few minutes later, when they had found a place to sit on one of the wool bales, that she was able to ask Martin the question that was burning a hole in her mind.

'What did you mean about Jan having second thoughts, Martin?'

'I had a letter from her—which is unusual to begin with. She's going to fly over here before I leave, and as I can't believe it's out of sisterly affection for me, I conclude she's weighed up the attractions of Paul Howard against those of Steve Gascoyne to the latter's advantage. In fact, I rather think she wants her ring back.'

Oh God! Ellis felt sick. Jan was coming back. She had felt it in her bones it was going to happen, but it didn't make it any easier to bear. Already in imagination she was suffering the embarrassment of having Jan find her here.

Unaware of the tumult in her heart, Martin went on, 'I heard from Dad too, by the way. He mentioned you hadn't written and wondered when you were coming home. I hope you're not going back, Ellis. If Jan gets married, he can pay someone to look after him—he can afford it. You've done more than your share of that.'

Ellis could do no more than give him a sickly smile and try to pretend she was enjoying her meal, though she'd eaten scarcely more than a mouthful of it, succulent though it was.

Presently Martin asked her, 'By the way, where's Charlie's wife? She's not here, is she?'

'She's gone to Melbourne for a break,' Ellis said reluctantly. 'She'll be back any time now ... When are you leaving, Martin?' she added hurriedly before he could ask her any more questions.

'I don't know. In a week—ten days. I'd like to get in

a bit more fishing before I leave, and it depends on Jan
as well. I'd like to know what she's up to. What are your
plans? It's no wonder you look so threadbare if
Leanne's been away while shearing was on.'

'It hasn't been so bad,' she said uncomfortably. But
I've had just about enough. I—I may go when Leanne
comes back.'

'Very wise,' said Martin. 'Why don't you spend a
week at the hotel in Whitemark with me and Jan, when
she comes?'

She shook her head. 'I'll probably be gone before
Jan comes.'

'Really? You sound quite positively positive. But
don't go back to Dad, will you? He must make himself
independent of you two girls ... I'm as dry as a bone,'
he remarked then. 'Would you like some beer, Ellis?'

She grimaced. 'No, thank you. But you go ahead and
get some for yourself.'

He nodded, and promising to be right back, he left
her.

Ellis stayed where she was, then glanced uneasily in
Steve's direction and saw he was in the act of handing
over his duties as barbecue chef to a husky middle-aged
man she remembered Martin introducing to her as Bob
Mussett. The next moment he came towards her, and
there was something decidedly menacing in his broad
muscular shoulders in the checked shirt. The silver
streak in his hair glinted in the light from the unshaded
light bulbs, and Ellis sent him a nervous smile, then
glanced guiltily at the uneaten meat on her plate.

'Not hungry, Ellis?' His eyes raked over her and he
reached out and took her plate from her, setting it
down on the wool bale beside her. 'Stop playing with it.
You can come outside for a walk with me. I want to

talk to you—but not in this hubbub.'

She bit her lip nervously and looked for Martin, but a group of men obstructed her view across the shed.

'Forget about Martin,' he said, aware of what she was doing. 'You've spent enough time with your cousin.' He took her roughly by the arm and hauled her to her feet, and perforce she had to go ahead of him to the steps and outside.

'What do you want to talk to me about?' she demanded, when at last, having reached a place well away from the lights and noise of the shed, he brought her to a halt with a jerk at her wrist that twisted her round to face him.

'First I want to tell you I haven't been amused by your performance tonight. You've deliberately given everyone the idea that you're Martin Webster's girl-friend, haven't you?'

'That's not true,' she retorted, glad that the darkness hid her guilty looks. 'But anyhow, why should it matter? It's better than having them——' She faltered and her voice trailed off. She could see his cynical smile now that her eyes were becoming accustomed to the dark.

'Better than having them—speculate about you and me?' he finished for her. 'You can't say you weren't warned about that. Right at this moment there'll be one or two people wondering what you and I are doing out here in the dark together, by the way. And since I don't intend taking you back inside again, they'll pretty soon be aware they made a mistake in assigning you to Martin Webster.'

She drew back from him a little. 'You're despicable, Steve Gascoyne! Thank goodness I shan't have to put up with you much longer!'

'What do you mean by that?' His eyes bored down into her in the darkness.

'Shearing's over. You said I could go.'

'I said we'd discuss it—but I've changed my mind about that,' he said. 'I gave you your way once and I regret it. I'm not going to be so agreeable this time.'

Ellis's heart was beating fast. She *had* to go, and yet she felt this crazy weakness in her, almost as if she could give in here and now, and say the fateful words, 'I'll marry you'. But he didn't love her. Besides which, Jan was coming back. And Jan always got what she wanted. She wouldn't stand a chance against Jan. It was funny, that—to think of the two of them vying for a man who didn't love either of them. Did Jan feel about him as she did, she wondered, or was it the fact that he was a Koolong Gascoyne that attracted her?

She raised her head, aware that a few seconds had gone by and she hadn't spoken. With an effort she told him, 'I don't want to stay.'

'Why not? What have you and Martin been talking about tonight?'

'I—I don't know what you mean,' she stammered.

'Is your boy-friend available again, that's what I mean,' he said. 'Do you want to go back to him?'

Ellis searched her mind wildly for an answer. Of course she didn't want to go back to Paul—but it would be an excuse. She said confusedly, 'Going back is not —not as easy as all that, is it?'

'I wouldn't know,' he said dryly. 'It's not part of my philosophy as a rule ... *Do* you want to go back to Paul, Ellis?'

She gazed at him helplessly, her breath coming fast, and the next minute she was in his arms. He held her hard against him, but he didn't kiss her, and she could feel her own heart beating but not his, close though she was to him. But of course, he didn't have a heart, she thought madly. He had slid a hand under her blouse and she could feel its warmth against her bare back as he looked down into her face. She had the strange feeling he could see her face as clearly as if it were day, and her eyes dwelt on his own features—the dark inscrutable eyes, the wide mouth, the lips curved in a line that was so often cynical and cruel, though in this light she didn't know what it was. Not for the first time she wondered about the place he called Disillusion Island, and a thousand unanswered questions came into her mind. She knew so little about him and about his reasons for despising women. She wished he had talked to her more about himself——

Her thoughts suddenly flew into confusion. His fingers were gently caressing her bare skin, and soon all she was conscious of was the fact that their two bodies were pressed burningly together and that he wanted her.

And that she wanted him.

Afraid, she twisted, trying uselessly to withdraw from him, knowing how terribly easy it would be for him to persuade her to give in to him right now. And he knew it too—he knew she was weakening.

She said in a low husky voice, 'Please—let me go.'

He released her slowly, then caught her hands in his. 'You've answered my question, Ellis. You want to stay here with me, don't you?'

She lowered her head and pulled her hands away from him, then tremblingly straightened her blouse, pushing it back under the waistband of her skirt. Her cheeks were hot and her senses were whirling. When he spoke to her like that, she was so terribly tempted.

She wished insanely that she'd agreed to his proposition in the first place—married him, taken a chance. But she hadn't wanted it then, and now it was too late. Jan was coming back to—to kiss and make up. An engagement ring would mean nothing to Jan, who anyway would be furious to find Ellis here at all, and could easily accuse her of sneaking in behind her back—trying to steal her man——

'Well?' Steve persisted, and she said nervily, 'We've been over all that. I—I happen to believe in love, even if you don't.'

'That's no disadvantage,' he said slowly. 'If a woman believes in love, and a man makes her happy, she'll learn to love him. Give yourself a bit more time, Ellis —stay on as long as you need. I want you.'

'You want a woman in your bed,' she said tremblingly. All he thought of when she talked of love was that she would come to love him. He didn't see that she wanted to be loved too, and she remembered what she had heard Leanne say, and repeated it now. 'Women are only useful for breeding—that's how you see it. There's no point in my staying here.'

He said dryly, 'I could persuade you if I wanted— right here and now. But I'll let you sleep on it. Remember this, though—my wife will have everything she wants—everything she asks for.'

Ellis raised her head. 'Everything? You mean you'd go and live at Koolong?'

'Oh, I don't think you'd try to talk me into that, Ellis,' he said with a crooked smile.

No, she wouldn't. And that, she thought bleakly, was the one and only advantage she had over Jan. It was hardly a reflection that comforted her.

A moment later Martin came towards them from the direction of the shearing shed.

'Are you all right, Ellis?' he asked rather sharply, seeing her standing in the dark with Steve.

Steve answered for her, his voice irritated. 'For God's sake, of course she's all right! But she's not going back inside. She's had enough of that rowdy lot in the shed. I'm taking her home.'

'I can do that,' said Martin.

Steve completely ignored his offer. 'Tell my brother to take over from Bob Mussett, will you?' he ordered briefly. 'Come along, Ellis.'

Ellis knew it was no use protesting. She told Martin, 'I'll be in touch. It was lovely seeing you. Goodnight,' and almost before he had time to reply Steve had taken her arm and they were heading for his car.

During the few minutes it took to drive to the homestead, she sat beside him shivering slightly and wondering if he'd want to come inside with her. Surely—surely he'd want to go back to the shearing shed. Yet she wouldn't put it past him to stay away—to let it be noticed that he and she had disappeared together.

As soon as he pulled up on the driveway she had her fingers on the door handle. 'Thank you, Steve. I'll be all right now.'

To her infinite relief he let her go, merely telling her, 'Think over what I've said—and remember I want you to stay just as much as I did when I first brought you here.'

'I'll remember,' she said dryly, and left him to run up the steps and in at the open front door. Why couldn't everything be different? she wondered despairingly, as she went upstairs. Why couldn't he *love* her? Why couldn't he at the very least *say* that he loved her—pretend to it? She could give in to him then without the feeling of shame she'd have otherwise. If it hadn't been for Martin's news about Jan, she might have been tempted to stay. But she could imagine Jan's reaction on finding her here. It would be—shattering. She knew she couldn't face it.

Well, she didn't have to, she reminded herself a little later as she got into bed. There was nothing in the world to stop her leaving long before Jan came.

Astonishingly, she fell asleep quickly, then woke in the small hours of the morning, disturbed by the soft sounds of Steve and Charlie coming up the stairs to bed.

I'll tell him in the morning, she thought. There's not a thing he can do to stop me from going.

She was as determined as ever to stick to her decision when she woke in the morning. It was after nine and the room was hot, and for a moment she lay luxuriating in the feeling that she didn't have to spend the day preparing meals for the shearers. All that was over.

In fact, almost the whole of her experience at Warrianda was behind her. It remained only to decide which day she would leave and arrange for a taxi to take her to the airfield. She'd go to her uncle's home and start looking for a job from there.

She went downstairs with the feeling she was about to attend her own execution. But only Charlie was in the breakfast room, sitting at the table drinking tea and looking rather gloomy.

'Where's Steve?' Ellis asked, pulling out a chair and then reaching for the teapot.

'He's fixing the generator. It refused to go this morning—too much of a load last night. Did you want to see him particularly?'

Ellis shook her head. Steve didn't air his affairs—didn't answer questions. She too could be discreet, and after all, it was between them.

'I had a letter from Lee yesterday,' Charlie said
moodily when a few minutes had passed in silence. 'She
reckons she won't come back if Steve doesn't get a
woman to live in and take charge.'

'Oh.' Ellis looked at his unhappy face and felt a
pang of sympathy for him. 'But he will get someone,
won't he?'

Charlie shrugged and stared at his empty cup. 'My
brother's an odd sort of a guy, Ellis. In most ways he's
the salt of the earth, but when it comes to women he's
hard—too hard for Lee. He's not going to get a housekeeper. He says Lee can come home first. Well, Lee
can be stubborn too, and she says she won't come. The
thing is, it's Steve's house, and I don't have the money
to pay a housekeeper anyway. So you can guess where
that leaves me.'

Ellis frowned. With shearing over, she couldn't see
that there was anything Leanne couldn't handle, but
on the other hand, it did seem Steve was being unnecessarily harsh, particularly if his brother's marriage
was at stake. She said at last, 'Charlie, why don't you
leave here and go to Koolong? That's what Leanne
wants, isn't it? And you must know practically everything about sheep raising now.'

'I need to know a whole lot more before I can hold
my own at Koolong. The others have been in the game
for years—Colin, and Di's husband as well. I was the
rebel of the family, I'm afraid. I didn't want to know
about sheep farming when I finished my education. I
lived at Koolong a while and drove everyone mad, then
I shot off to Melbourne and got through a whole heap
of money doing nothing.' He sent Ellis a wry grimace.
'By the time I came to my senses, Colin didn't want me

around the place, but Steve took me on here. I still have to prove I have the right to go back where I belong—this place doesn't belong to the Gascoyne family, you know, Grandfather left it to Steve.'

'I know,' Ellis said slowly. 'But—but doesn't Leanne understand?'

'She doesn't see it the way I do,' Charlie said broodingly. 'Her heart's set on Koolong. It's partly my fault —I let her know when I asked her to marry me that we'd live there eventually. We'd make out in the meantime if she and Steve got on together better, but he's so determined she should accept everything and shut up that it gets her down.'

'Why is he like that, Charlie?' Ellis asked without really meaning to.

Charlie frowned and moved his cup a little, then glanced up at her. 'I don't usually discuss Steve's private life, Ellis, but—well, you're a nice girl, and maybe it will help if I answer your question. You see, he took a pretty nasty knock when he was in his early twenties. I was a kid away at school and Colin was still at university—and Steve was working for Father on Koolong. He got engaged to a girl and then shortly before the wedding he discovered she was pregnant. The man was——' He stopped and chewed at his lower lip, then resumed, 'It was someone she'd known before she met Steve.'

'That must have been terrible for him,' Ellis breathed. 'He—he didn't marry her, of course?'

'No. The general idea seemed to be that she'd set out to win Steve because of Koolong. It was pretty disillusioning for him. I suppose he'd really been in love with her, but it seemed she didn't care tuppence for him—except that he was the eldest Gascoyne, the one who'd be running the show. Steve cleared out and more or less made a hermit of himself on that island he owns. He didn't want any more to do with women—I guess he didn't trust them. He worked like mad—bought cattle, built himself a bungalow, added a few rough comforts. I reckon he was all set to spend the rest of his life there when Grandfather began to fail and he came over to Warrianda to help the old man—who left the property to him, instead of to Colin, as he'd originally intended.'

'I see. And he doesn't ever think of going back to Koolong?' Ellis asked.

'That would be the last place on earth he'd go to,' Charlie said forcibly, then before Ellis could ask why he was so vehement, he continued, 'So that's why he has this thing about a woman marrying a man for what she can get out of him—and he takes it out on Lee.' He pushed back his chair, then instead of standing up, he asked Ellis unexpectedly, 'Look, Ellis, can I tell Lee when I ring her tonight that you'll still be here if she comes back? It's the only way I can think of to persuade her to come. I'm at my wits' end, as you can imagine.'

Ellis stared at him. She'd made up her mind she was leaving, but how could she refuse Charlie? It took her only a second to make up her mind, and tell him yes, she'd be here.

'You're an angel,' said Charlie, immediately looking a whole lot happier. He went off then to see how Steve was making out with the generator, and Ellis finished her tea thoughtfully. She was committed to stay now, but she wasn't going to let Steve think it was on his account. She was going to tell him why she was staying —and as well, she'd tell him what she thought of him.

Her opportunity didn't come till that night when she was cooking the dinner, as Steve had spent most of the day getting some sheep ready for trucking to Lady Barron.

He looked into the kitchen to tell her, 'Come into the office, Ellis, and I'll let you have your pay cheque.'

Ellis looked at him coolly—or tried to do so, but found she couldn't and had to look away again. She was becoming far too addicted to dwelling on his appearance. He stood aside for her to go through the door past him, and she pulled off the apron she was wearing and went ahead of him to the office. Then, when he had handed her her cheque across a very formidable desk, she said firmly, 'I'd better tell you, Steve—I made up my mind last night that I wouldn't stay here any longer.'

His eyes flickered for an instant and she thought it was with annoyance, but before he could comment she hurried on, 'I am staying though—but not because of you. I'm staying because Charlie asked me to.'

He frowned. 'Charlie asked you? What do you mean?'

'Leanne won't come back unless you hire a woman to do the housework. I don't pretend to know why you won't, but that's why I'm staying. *You* mightn't care if your brother's marriage breaks up because of your— your high-handedness, but I'm not going to be a party to it.'

'Very noble of you,' he said after a moment. 'But I'm not going to hire *you* to do the housework, Ellis. I hate the sight of you in that damned apron. Lee will cook and clean and keep house when she comes back, because that's the way it should be. She's not here as a guest, and if she had any sort of a conscience she'd

feel in honour bound to do her share of the work here.
If Charlie lets her get away with selfish behaviour then
he's a fool. So I'm not going to argue with you about
Leanne. I know the situation better than you do, and I
know she needs a firm hand.'

'Isn't that for her husband to decide?' Ellis asked,
flushing at his tone.

'And isn't it for me to decide whether or not I'm
going to engage a housekeeper?' he retorted.

Ellis knew she was defeated on that point and she
grimaced and turned to go when he said, 'Ellis——'

'Yes?'

'You have got the situation clear, haven't you? Your
name's no longer on the wages sheet at Warrianda. As
from now, you're my guest. You can help Lee with her
chores if you want to, but she will be responsible for
getting things done, and she will be responsible for
anything left undone.'

'You're very hard,' said Ellis, and when she went
back to the kitchen, she thought what an idiot she was.
She couldn't solve Charlie's and Leanne's problems—
they'd have to do that themselves. She was only going
to cause trouble for herself by staying here.

That night she wrote a letter to Jan, putting the
Warrianda address at the top. 'Dear Jan—You can see
from the address on this letter where I am, and I guess
you're really surprised. I've been too busy to write before as I've just finished a job as shearers' cook, and
now I'm staying on to help with the housekeeping.
Martin says you're coming over to Flinders again, so
next time we meet it will most likely be here. Give my
love to Uncle Bill. I hope you haven't found it too much
of a bore looking after him—he's very easy to get on
with, isn't he? Please remember me to Paul.' She

signed it, 'Affectionately, Ellis,' then resolutely sealed it up in an envelope. Jan would fume when she read it —but at least she'd know Ellis was here—she'd be prepared.

CHAPTER NINE

On Monday, Ellis managed to get the old car going and went to Whitemark to post her letter. Charlie had rung Leanne, and she had agreed to come back at the end of the week. Meanwhile, Ellis was a mass of nerves, terrified that Jan would turn up before she'd got her letter, wondering why she'd been so silly as to say she'd stay. Yet it would have been on her conscience if she'd refused.

That week, the sale sheep were trucked off to Lady Barron from where they'd be taken by barge to Welshpool, and activity at Warrianda slowed down. The day Leanne was to arrive, Steve asked Ellis to come to Lady Barron with him, and she agreed, telling herself it would give Charlie and Lee a chance to conduct their reunion privately. Yet she knew very well that the mere thought of being alone with Steve again excited her. He had been pleasant to her during the last few days, but they hadn't had a moment alone. Evenings, the three of them had talked—about music, politics, books, country life—everything under the sun—and she'd found the conversation agreeable and stimulating. Looking at Steve, listening to him talk, she had wondered about him a lot. He had a fine face, except for that hard cynicism about his eyes and mouth. When he relaxed, it disappeared and he was undeniably handsome, and very very attractive, and she fell more and more deeply in love with him as the days went by.

The day they drove to Lady Barron was blue and sunny, and after they'd passed Mount Strzelecki, Steve

took the coast road that ran along by Adelaide Bay, so
that they could enjoy the sight of the black swans and
the pelicans sailing along over the clear green water. At
the jetty in Lady Barron there were a couple of crayfish boats as well as the big barge that was taking sheep
and cattle and other goods to Welshpool on the mainland.

They left the car and walked along by the yards
where the stock was held before being directed into a
narrow race that led on to the barge and the temporary
pens there. Ellis loitered, watching some cattle being
hunted along the race. One huge beast, its bulk reaching almost from one side to the other, refused to budge
and had to be prodded most ungently before it lum-
bered on unwillingly. Steve meanwhile had sauntered
on and was talking to the captain, but he rejoined Ellis
after a moment and presently they went back to the car
and drove to the top of Vinegar Hill. From there they
could see away across Franklin Sound to Cape Barren
Island.

Steve pointed out the wreck of the barque, the
Farsund, her hulk still wholly visible and looking almost seaworthy though she had gone aground in 1912.

'There are over a hundred wrecks in the waters
round the Furneaux Group,' he told Ellis. 'That's
mainly due to the Roaring Forties, though it's said that
some ships were lured to their destruction by adven-
turers who set themselves up here as sealers in the early
days. There's no more sealing nowadays, and even
muttonbirding is declining. I went after muttonbirds
with my grandfather a few times when I was a kid.
Moonbirds, the old man called them,' he added with a
faint smile. 'They come down to Bass Strait in thou-
sands in September, to clean out the burrows they used
the year before. Then they go out to sea and come back

late November to lay their eggs. The parents feed the chicks so well on the food they gather from the sea that the fledglings are as fat as butter by April, when they're left to fend for themselves. That's when the birders harvest them—scoop the helpless creatures out of their burrows. If you're experienced, you can tell by the warmth just inside the burrow whether you're likely to get a chick or find yourself mixed up with a snake.'

Ellis listened interestedly, and found herself remembering the night he said she reminded him of a moonbird chick—when she'd gone to his suite wearing her black skirt and her high-necked blouse. He said into her thoughts, 'I don't know that you're really as helpless as one of those chicks, you know—I think you're pretty well able to fend for yourself. But I don't have any intention of scooping you up and eating you, my dear.' He put his arm around her shoulders and added softly, 'I wouldn't do that to you, Ellis. I'd put you in a golden cage.'

It was an odd and unexpected thing for him to say even though his voice was a trifle sardonic, and Ellis felt confused. He'd been—different to her lately. If he could have been like that in Hobart, instead of so hard and cynical. And it was all because of that other girl, years and years ago.

She asked him musingly, 'Where's your island, Steve? Can you see it from here?'

'No, it's some distance away. I'll take you there one day—it has a lot of attractions despite its name. Would you like that?'

He spoke as if she'd be here for some time yet, and again she was disconcerted, because she was quite positive she wouldn't. Once Jan came, everything would blow up. She said a little uneasily, 'I'm interested. Tell me about it. Why—why did you go there?'

He shrugged his broad shoulders. 'I had my reasons. I wanted to get away from the world—come to terms with the fact that life wasn't a fairy story.'

'What did you do there?' she asked after a moment, and knew she badly wanted him to tell her about it, as if it might prove something—that he trusted her, for instance.

'I ran cattle and I built a house,' he said disappointingly.

'You used to live at Koolong, didn't you?' she persisted. 'Why—why did you leave there?'

He looked at her quizzically. 'I'll tell you the story of my life some day, Ellis—but not till I've persuaded you to marry me.'

She bit her lip. 'That will be never,' she said, her voice low.

He raised one eyebrow and said dryly, 'You've given me a new weapon, Ellis. Women are said to be very curious ... At all events, it's time we collected the car you're to drive home.'

'What?' She looked at him stupidly.

'Oh, didn't I tell you? I ordered a car from Launceston the day you flew over to Flinders with me. It's at last arrived—on the barge today. You didn't think I'd want you to go on struggling with that old heap you've been using, did you?'

Ellis stared at him, her face paling. Was he telling her he'd bought her a new car? But that was impossible—it was—crazy. She said uncertainly, 'You—you mean you bought it for Leanne——'

'I mean no such thing. I don't buy new cars for Leanne. That's up to Charlie. The car's for you.'

She shook her head. 'But I'm not staying—it's only

because I promised Charlie——'

'Ellis!' His eyes had darkened and he took her by the shoulders and shook her gently. 'What's the matter with you? Who do you imagine you're fooling? You can be happy here with me—a thousand times happier than with some man who starts up an affair with another woman at the drop of a hat.'

His eyes had gone to her mouth and she said shakily, 'You—*you* seem to start new affairs at the drop of a hat. Jan—me——'

'Oh, forget Jan,' he said impatiently. 'She's off the scene.'

'Have you forgotten her?' she challenged, aware, even if he was not, that soon Jan would be well and truly back on the scene.

'It's comon sense,' he said briefly. 'She's like Leanne —she wants to carry the stockwhip. No woman dictates to me.'

Ellis was silent, but she drew away from him. It was terrible to be so besotted over a man who didn't even pretend to love you—or anyone else for the matter of that. All he wanted was a woman who'd submit to him —and of course, share his bed. Sharing his bed would be no problem to Jan—but she wouldn't submit to living here, and Ellis was positive she must have some tricky plan in mind that she meant to carry out when she came back. With Ellis, it was the other way about. Living at Warrianda would suit her perfectly well, but she wouldn't—couldn't—share his bed unless he loved her.

Her head lowered, she began to move back to the car. The *new* car would do for Jan, she thought despairingly, then gasped as Steve's arms came round her from behind and he pulled her back against his body and moved his mouth softly against her neck near the lobe of her ear.

She caught her breath and pulled away from him sharply. 'Don't!'

He said nothing, but he was scowling as he got into the car beside her a minute later, and she thought wryly, Jan wouldn't have pulled away. He was soon going to discover he hadn't forgotten Jan after all.

The new car was a light blue Mazda 121 with pale silvery grey upholstery, and it was a dream to drive. 'My wife will have everything.' Ellis remembered the words as she followed the glistening white road towards Warrianda, not attempting to keep up with Steve who had sped ahead.

Once back at the homestead she parked the car, feeling a little surprised that Leanne hadn't come outside to welcome her and look at the new car. It entered her mind as she went inside that Leanne might be sulking over the fact the car was not for her, unless she was busy in the kitchen. Steve had made it very plain that he was going to insist that Leanne should do the work about the house, and that Ellis should only help.

From the hall, she caught the sound of Steve's voice. He was in the office, and she wondered if he had Leanne on the mat already over something, or if he was merely talking to Charlie. After a brief hesitation she went upstairs. She'd have a wash, then tidy herself up and come down to the kitchen. It was well after six, and if he was lecturing Leanne it was possible she hadn't even started to get dinner.

She had brushed out her dark gold hair and was standing in front of the mirror feeling rather tensed up when Steve came to the door. She turned swiftly, and was disconcerted by the look on his face; it was so—proprietorial.

His green gaze took her in slowly from head to toe. She had put on a long cotton voile skirt and matching top, with the idea of giving a festive air to Leanne's return, and she knew the flimsy material accentuated her slender waist and the line of her bosom. There was colour in her cheeks from the day in the open and that, combined with the light tan she had acquired, made her look particularly fit.

After a long pause, Steve said slowly, 'You grow more beautiful by the hour, Ellis. But I didn't come up-stairs to remark on the obvious, I've something else to tell you. There was a message from Charlie when I came home that Leanne's been taken to hospital, and he's taken the plane over to Melbourne. I've just been speaking to Mrs Burnett—Leanne's mother—on the phone. The doctor diagnosed acute appendicitis and operated at once.'

'Oh, poor Leanne! Is she all right?' Ellis breathed out.

'She's getting on fine—she has the best doctors look-ing after her, you may be sure. It could be fortunate she was on the mainland,' he added, and somehow, as he spoke, Ellis suddenly realised that now she and he were completely alone in the house, and she felt her pulses quicken nervously.

'When—will Charlie be back?' she asked jerkily.

'When he's ready to come,' said Steve. 'He can stay with his wife as long as he wishes, so don't look at me like that. I'm not heartless, whatever you may think.'

Ellis bit her lip and looked rather wildly round the room. She had been thinking of herself this time, not of Leanne, and crazily her thoughts had gone to that other room where Steve slept—in a bed even bigger than this one. It hadn't even entered her head that Steve might insist his brother should come back immediately, and her cheeks were crimson and then pale as she said stiffly, 'I—I didn't for a moment think you'd expect Charlie to leave Leanne.'

'You didn't? Well, that's good news,' he said, and she turned away hastily from the look in his eyes and said hurriedly, 'I—I was just going downstairs to see about dinner.'

'For two,' he said, and her nerves leapt.

But he didn't touch her as she moved past him through the doorway, and she heard him going into his bedroom as she made her way down the stairs.

In the kitchen she tried to consider the position calmly, but the fact that Steve had behaved himself so well lately didn't make it much better. She still didn't know what to expect from him—particularly if they were alone. The fact was plain from this afternoon's exchange that he hadn't by any means given up the idea of making her his wife, and as she prepared vegetables to accompany grilled chops, she came to the conclusion that the only thing to do was to move out of his house—as soon as possible ...

She was tense and nervous over dinner. There was a disturbing intimacy in sitting at the long narrow table with him with the sky dark outside and silence all around them—except for the soft music he had put on the cassette recorder. It was as if only the two of them existed in the whole world—herself and this handsome virile man with the enigmatic eyes and the dark hair with its dramatic streak of silver, and she glanced almost fearfully at the long curving mouth whose touch she knew so well and so much desired. Tonight he wore dark pants and a soft cream shirt with a narrow rolled collar that showed up his suntanned skin and the whiteness of his teeth, and she found it hard to keep her eyes off him.

They didn't talk much, and after they had eaten she took his coffee into the sitting room, then, leaving her own there, murmured a vague excuse and once outside the room went quickly upstairs. She would take the new car and go to the hotel in Whitemark—sneak out without telling him, because she felt quite positive he would try to stop her from going—and all too likely would succeed.

In her room she changed quickly into pants and shirt, then proceeded to pack a few things in one of her suitcases. She could hear music floating up the stairs, and she thought that, with luck, he wouldn't hear the car. It wasn't as if it was the noisy old thing that she customarily drove.

She had reached the foot of the stairs when Steve appeared in the hallway from the sitting room. Ellis stood stock still and stared at him, feeling as guilty as if she'd been caught out doing something thoroughly dishonest—which in a way she had.

'I wondered what you were up to when you disappeared,' he said dryly. 'What are you trying to do? Run away before I seduce you? Haven't I already convinced you I'm not going to do that? It wasn't Charlie's presence that prevented it from happening, you know —I've had plenty of opportunity——'

Ellis felt an absolute fool. But all the same, she didn't trust him, and she trusted herself still less, if he only knew it. She said shakily but determinedly, 'There's just no point in my being here now. Leanne won't be back for a while, and I—I only stayed on to please Charlie.'

'Haven't we already disagreed about that?' He came towards her purposefully as he spoke and she shrank back against the wall, her heart beating fast. His voice, his look, unnerved her, and she was intensely aware

that he had only to take her in his arms for all her reso-
lution to melt away. But there was no escaping him,
and in a split second it had happened. She heard the
slight thud as her suitcase hit the floor and then her
body was brought into contact with Steve's. His mouth
was against hers and she was twisting futilely against his
strength and feeling, second by second, her self-control
slipping, her desire to escape from him fading out like
the lights in a theatre as the music begins.

And now for her too the music was beginning, its
rhythm pounding through her blood as she helplessly
—willingly—let him gather her closer and closer. His
hand found her breast and she clung to him, feeling the
warmth of his body spreading through her in ripples
right to her very heart. When he took his lips away from
hers so that they could both draw breath, his head was
still close to hers and their eyes were locked in a long
unbreakable exchange. His eyes were not emeralds tonight, they were not hard and cynical—they were
fragments of the watery jewel that was the sea, sparked
with light, deep enough to drown in, enticing enough
—and Ellis was drowning—drowning——

'Steve——' she heard herself whisper as again he
crushed her to him, and she knew with a shudder that
was part fear, part anticipation, that if he wanted her
now he could have her—he could carry her up the
stairs to his bed and make love to her all night long.
And after that—after that——

She should at that point have dragged herself away
from him, but she couldn't. She was beyond making
any kind of moral effort.

It was he who brought the passions that were rising
between them to an end eventually. Even while she was
silently imploring, 'Don't let me go—love me—make
me yours——' she heard him swear beneath his breath,

and the next instant, stunned and helpless, she found the embrace had come to an abrupt and cruel end.

Steve picked up her suitcase, took her roughly by the arm, and propelled her towards the door.

'You'd better go, Ellis—you were quite right, you'll be safer in Whitemark. I'll take you to the hotel.'

Ellis wanted to protest, to say no, but that would be to agree to everything that would follow. And she just couldn't see Steve marrying her once Jan turned up— Jan wouldn't allow it.

Neither of them said anything further and she went with him on shaking legs to his car. It was no use offering to drive herself—the Mazda was his, not hers, and besides, the way she was feeling now she wouldn't trust herself to drive a hundred yards with safety. As she sat by his side and they followed the long white road through the darkness, she prayed silently that he would tell her he loved her. Oh God, if only he would say that then nothing else would matter in the whole world.

But he didn't tell her he loved her, and she knew why. Love simply didn't enter his scheme of things. He didn't trust women—they were cheats. The wonder was that he was letting her go instead of——

In the darkness she closed her eyes and drew a quivering breath. If she had never been grateful to Steve Gascoyne before, she should feel grateful to him now. He could have done anything to her, back at the house, and she'd have regretted it bitterly afterwards.

When he pulled up outside the hotel in Whitemark he turned in the seat and asked her soberly, 'Will you be all right, Ellis?'

She nodded, but didn't speak and she didn't even look at him. Shame and embarrassment swept over her in waves and she thanked heaven that the light from the hotel didn't fall on her face. She climbed unsteadily out of the car and when he set her suitcase down on the footpath, she told him, 'Don't come in with me. I can —manage everything for myself.'

'All right, Ellis,' he agreed. Then with a brief goodnight, he got back into the car and as she went into the hotel she heard him drive away.

Fortunately, she didn't see Martin, and she didn't ask for him. All she wanted now was to hide herself away in the hotel bedroom and wake to find it had all been a dream. But of course she didn't do that. She lay awake, her body burning with longing for Steve. Over and over she wished he hadn't let her go—that he had done what she had imagined, taken her to his bed and made love to her. She was wishing it still when she fell asleep at last, the warmth of tears on her cheeks.

When morning came she was pale and there were shadows under her eyes, but she was in full control of her senses again. She wanted never to have to see Steve Gascoyne again, and she wished she had brought all her possessions with her instead of just the one suitcase containing a few things. She decided to ask Martin to come with her to Warrianda, and then she could take the plane in the afternoon—to Melbourne, she decided despairingly.

But when she went down to breakfast and enquired about Martin, it was only to be told that he had left early that morning for Burnett Lagoon. Immediately she felt exposed—vulnerable—like some little sea creature without its shell. Or like—yes, like the little moonbird chick Steve had once called her. Then presently she calmed down. She'd hire a car and drive out to Burnett Lagoon and find Martin.

In a very short time she was on her way, but the drive took longer than she had expected and the last part of it was decidedly rough. Then when the great sheet of water appeared, there was not a sign of Martin or of any other human being. Ellis sat in the car and realised how rashly and foolishly she had acted. Martin must have moved on to somewhere else. She shouldn't have wasted time coming to look for him, and now she'd have to do what she should have done in the first place —drive to Warrianda for her things and then go to the airport. After all, Steve couldn't stop her. She was being melodramtic.

Instead of going back through Whitemark, she decided to cut across the island, even though she had no map, but eventually it took her longer that way because she was soon hopelessly lost. It wasn't till she recognised Mount Killiecrankie that she knew where she was, and finally she reached Warrianda just in time to see another car disappearing along the white road— a taxi, she realised later, but at the time all she knew was that it was not Steve's car.

His car was not in the driveway either, she found a moment later as she drove up to the house, and though she told herself she was in luck, a deeper part of her being was desolated. Not even to be able to say good- bye—— Yet it was safer that way. She parked the hire car under a red flowering gum, and for the first time realised she couldn't catch the plane after all. It was well after lunch time, and she was desperately hungry. She'd had a very light breakfast and she hadn't brought even as much as a bar of chocolate with her. She went quickly into the house, wondering nervously if she'd get herself something to eat in the kitchen before she went up to pack. Then, just inside the front door, she stopped short, her heart pounding.

Jan Webster had come out of the sitting room and she stood and stared at Ellis, her beautiful black-lashed grey eyes flaring into anger.

'Where's Steve?' she snapped out, looking over Ellis's shoulder.

Ellis swallowed, her throat dry. She moved her hands in a vague gesture implying she didn't know, and Jan's glance moved sharply and disparagingly over her.

'What on earth have you been doing to yourself?' she demanded. 'Where did you get those clothes—and that watch——' With a few quick steps she came closer and seized Ellis by the wrist, staring unbelievingly at the little jewelled watch Jake had given her. Then without warning she raised her hand and slapped Ellis's cheek with one stingingly swift blow. 'You —you *sneaky* little beast—chasing after Steve behind my back! What's going on? What's happened between you and him? And where is everyone? Where's Leanne? Where's Charlie?'

Ellis was still reeling from that blow, and she could hardly follow the questions that followed each other like rifle shots. For the first time in her life she saw real hatred looking back at her from someone's eyes, and she stared back at Jan as if she had been struck dumb.

Her silence seemed to make Jan angrier than ever, but this time she didn't slap her. She darted up the stairs.

'I'm going to see for myself just where you've been sleeping!' Ellis heard her hiss.

Ellis leaned against the wall for a few seconds, breathing deeply, then with an effort she too went up the stairs and was just in time to receive an armful of her own clothes in her face as Jan hurled them through the door.

'You and your housekeeping!' Jan shouted furiously. 'Where did you get all these expensive things, I'd like to know? From Steve, of course—didn't you?' Her voice rose as she rushed back into the bedroom, and Ellis stood in the doorway watching as in a frenzy she began dragging the clothes from the wardrobe and flinging them around the room.

'Jan, don't,' Ellis begged, hating to see her lovely things so mistreated. 'It—it was true what I told you in my letter. I—I came here to cook for the shearers— to keep house——'

'As if I'd ever believe such lies!' Jan exclaimed. She threw a pair of shoes across the room. 'You never had clothes like this when you were in East Ivanhoe looking after Father. Don't tell *me* your creepy little stories about working here—I can imagine for myself what you're getting paid for and I know *exactly* why you came. Well, he won't marry you—don't fool yourself about that! He wants me, do you understand? And now I've decided to let him have his way over a little difference of opinion we had, he won't want you hanging around any more. You'd better pack up your clothes and get out now ... I'd like to know how you tricked Martin into keeping quiet about your being here!'

Watching her cousin, listening to her angry ranting, Ellis found she had lost her fear and was becoming deadly calm. She caught sight of her own reflection in the mirror—her face chalk white, except for one red spot on either cheek, and those dark shadows under her eyes.

'Jan,' she said quietly, 'if you'll listen I'll tell you— I'll explain——'

'I don't want to hear,' Jan snapped. She had asked all those questions, but now she didn't want to hear. 'It wouldn't be the truth—I wouldn't trust you this much,' she added, snapping her fingers. 'But believe me, Ellis, when I see Steve I'm going to tell him a few things about you that will upset your rosy apple cart.'

Ellis's eyes widened. 'What—what things?'

'About your affair with Paul—your *passionate* affair,' Jan snapped, her eyes sparkling with malice.

Ellis gasped. 'It—it wasn't passionate!'

'Oh, but it was,' Jan insisted. 'I heard all about it direct from him. You asked me in your letter to remember you to Paul, so I did—and that's when I heard all about how you were throwing yourself into his arms every opportunity you got. I'll tell Steve Father decided he couldn't have you in the house any longer, the things you were getting up to. Paul's girl-friend's back, by the way, if you're interested to know.'

'What—what girl-friend?' Ellis asked blankly, and Jan gave her an amused look.

'Oh, I thought you must have found out about her— she's been overseas for six months. They're being married next month. Well, I don't care—I have Steve,' she added viciously.

She dragged Ellis's suitcase on to the bed and opened it, then began to pile clothes into it any old how. Ellis watched her tremblingly for a moment, then stepped forward.

'Don't, Jan. I'll pack up. That's—that's why I came back.'

'What?' Jan spun round. 'You came *back*? What do you mean?'

'I—I left here last night,' said Ellis. 'Leanne had to go to hospital in Melbourne, and Charlie took the plane over to the mainland in the afternoon. It—it wasn't right I should be here alone with Steve, so he took me in to the hotel in Whitemark.'

Jan stared and then began to laugh. 'Oh, Ellis! You're incredible! You mean you wouldn't stay here

alone with him? But wasn't it a bit late? I mean—I
know Steve! You're such a phoney it's unreal. Why
not admit to what you've been up to? All those clothes
—that watch—they're *evidence*.' She had laughed, but
now the hatred and venom were back in her face and
Ellis drew back. Jan was so cruel—so domineering. Oh,
she had known there would be a shattering scene when
she came, but not that it would be anything like this, she
thought, surveying the shambles Jan had made of her
room. Deep in her heart she wished she had stayed
here last night—that somehow she had made Steve
hers. Yet Steve would never belong to any woman——

She stooped and began blindly gathering the things
Jan had scattered round the room, folding them
clumsily because her hands were shaking, and putting
them carefully into the suitcase on the bed.

'Jan, no matter what you think, nothing's happened
between me and Steve,' she said at last, in a choked
voice. 'You—you're quite wrong.'

Jan flung herself into an armchair and watched Ellis
through half-closed eyes.

'Nothing?' she sneered. 'You mean you haven't slept
with him? He hasn't made love to you? I'm afraid I
can't believe it—*you* wouldn't know how to hold such
a man at bay till you'd made your own terms.'

'It's true all the same,' Ellis said almost inaudibly.

Jan got up from the chair and gestured with a well
kept hand.

'Now come on, Ellis—all these clothes——' She
stopped and then exclaimed vehemently, 'Oh, my God!
Now I've got it—of course! Jake Armour! He's loaded,
isn't he? He bought you all this stuff in Hobart. Am I
right?' Ellis nodded, and Jan said tauntingly, 'And you
thought with this—this *bait*, you could hook a really big

fish, make Steve Gascoyne fall in love with you. But he didn't——'

Blindly, Ellis shook her head. Something inside her was dying, some tiny bud of hope that had been there until Jan came to take over. She blinked away tears and made herself look at Jan and ask, 'Will you—will Steve take you back? You—you quarrelled, didn't you?'

Jan flipped her fingers carelessly. 'We had a difference of opinion—and we've both been holding out for our own way. But we'll come to terms now I've taken the first step. Men are like that—they want the woman to give in and then they can be generous in a lordly way. All the same, I've taught him a lesson and I think I'll get what I want.'

'Do you mean about living at Koolong, Jan?' Ellis asked hesitantly. 'I really don't think he wants to live there.'

Jan, who had paced across the room to the mirror to stare at her own beautiful reflection, spun round. 'What do *you* know about it, Ellis? Once we're married I'll twist him round my little finger. Any woman who understands what makes the male sex tick can manipulate a man who loves her.'

She sounded so very sure of herself, but Ellis asked, 'How can you be so sure he loves you, Jan?'

Jan smiled a slow worldly smile. 'Ellis, when you've lain in a man's arms and made him as happy as a human being can be, you can tell if he loves you. Have you ever lain in your lover's arms after he's made love to you, Ellis?'

Ellis shook her head, embarrassed. 'No. And—and those things you said about Paul and me—you know they're not true.'

'Oh, who cares?' Jan said scornfully. 'I just want you to know I'm not short of ammunition if I should need it. If you behave yourself I *won't* need it—so see you do behave, Ellis, that's all. Because I mean to have Steve and nothing on earth is going to stop me. Paul Howard's going to see how little he meant to me.'

Ellis felt a shudder go through her. Jan was beautiful, but just now she looked so hard and calculating. She was a—cheat. The word flashed into Ellis's mind with a terrible clarity. Jan was one of those cheats that Steve hated—like the girl who transferred her affections to him because of Koolong. She said slowly but positively, 'Steve won't go back to Koolong, Jan. It reminds him too much of an unhappy love affair.'

Jan sat down on the end of the bed and smoothed back her dark hair. 'Ellis, I know all about that love affair, and it's just so ancient I'm not worried. He's the eldest son after all—Koolong is where he belongs and it's absurd that he should have been virtually banished by a girl like Patrice. His pride alone shouldn't allow it. *His* sons should be growing up at Koolong, not hers.'

Ellis listened without understanding. 'What—what do you mean, Jan? Who's Patrice?'

'Colin's wife, of course,' Jan explained. 'Didn't you know that? I heard the story years ago when I was holidaying with a school friend on their property in the Goulburn Valley. She's the girl Steve was going to marry—until he discovered she'd been sleeping with his brother. Colin's the one who should be here on Flinders Island—he was the one old Mr Gascoyne was making his heir, and when Patrice realised she'd be expected to live here if she married Colin, she switched her affections over to Steve—even before she'd met him. Then he found out she was pregnant, and like a fool he got out. He should have stayed put and be damned to them.'

Listening, Ellis felt appalled. So the girl Steve had

loved—the girl who had cheated him so cruelly—was
now married to his brother and living at Koolong. Colin
was the other man—the man Charlie hadn't named.
Everything began to fall into place, and she felt a new
and deep pain for Steve. To have been betrayed in that
way by any girl was bad enough, but in those particular circumstances he must have felt terribly bitter. She
began to understand why he suspected Leanne's love
for Charlie and was putting it to such tests.

Jan said lightly, 'We'll live on Flinders for a time
after we're married—but it won't be long before I've
convinced Steve he's been less than a man in letting
himself be driven out of Koolong. No man likes to be
thought weak, you know—particularly not a man like
Steve. He was young and impulsive then, I suppose,
and he'll soon see it's time to go back and take over—
for his children's sake. I just wouldn't have children,
anyhow, if they had to be brought up here instead of at
Koolong.'

Ellis felt repelled by her cousin's cunning, but she
knew there was not a thing she could do about it. If
she dared open her mouth, Jan would soon silence her
by telling Steve some malicious and untrue story about
Ellis and Paul Howard.

She told her cousin dully, as she packed the last of
her things into her suitcase, 'I'm going back to Whitemark now, Jan. I have a hire car outside. I—I meant
to take the plane today, but I missed it, and I'll have to
wait till tomorrow. Shall I tell Martin you're here if he
comes back to the hotel tonight?'

Jan walked to the door after Ellis, her silk skirt
swishing. 'Yes, tell him I'm here. He's expecting me.
Tell him I'm waiting to see Steve—that the situation is
now as it was before I left the island. I shall probably
stay here tonight, but I may come in to town with

Steve to see him tomorrow.'

Two minutes later Ellis and her luggage were in the hire car, and Jan was leaning in at the window and telling her, 'It's a pity you missed your plane, Ellis. Still, you'll be off tomorrow, won't you? Or do you want to stay to congratulate me and Steve?'

Ellis shook her head. 'I'd rather go back to Melbourne as I planned.'

'Very wise,' Jan said smugly. She leaned forward and kissed Ellis on the cheek. 'Goodbye, Ellis. I'm sure Father will be pleased to see you back.'

Ellis managed a smile as she started up the motor, but she felt she couldn't get away from Jan quickly enough. It was incredible that her cousin could be looking so calm and composed and beautiful. So short a time ago she had been in a vile temper—she had slapped Ellis's face, thrown her clothes about—behaved hatefully. Steve couldn't know the unpleasant side of her character. The calm and beautiful girl was the one he knew, the one he—loved.

And she, Ellis, had thought him incapable of love. But then she wasn't Jan.

CHAPTER TEN

MARTIN didn't appear in the hotel dining room that night, and Ellis ate alone, feeling lonelier than she had ever felt in her whole life. By now, Steve would be back at Warrianda from wherever he had spent the day, and he and Jan would have made up their quarrel. No doubt they would be in each other's arms by now.

Ellis dared not let her imagination carry her any further. She was burning with jealousy—a sensation she had never experienced before, and it was unbearable. She had thought she was jealous of Jan that night when Paul had stayed so late, but the emotion was weak and meaningless in comparison with what she felt now, and she realised that until now she hadn't known what jealousy was. She didn't know if it would make it better or worse to have Martin here now to keep her company. The last time they had met had been at the cut out, when Steve had very autocratically said he would take her home. She wondered what Martin had made of that, but she would never ask him now.

After dinner she walked restlessly through the small town and along the shore to where the jetty stretched a slender finger across the mysterious dark of the water. There were stars—a moon—and the water made soft sounds on the sand, and the air was full of the faint perfume of flowers. Ellis walked slowly, debating with herself about her future. It would be impossible to go back to Uncle Bill and take up the old life again, and neither did she want to go to Jake, to whom, she realised with a feeling of guilt, she had written only once since she had been at Warrianda. But she had a little money now—Jake had given her some and she had earned good wages as shearers' cook—and she would be able to support herself for a short time in Melbourne while she searched for work. That was as far ahead as she seemed capable of thinking just now.

When she went back to the hotel, she loitered about hoping there would be some message from Steve, but there was nothing, and there was no doubt in her heart that he had forgotten her. Otherwise, he'd have come.

Martin still didn't put in an appearance the following morning, and since it was Sunday, Ellis guessed he had probably stayed away fishing. It meant there would be no one to see her off, no one to say goodbye to her, and she put in a wretchedly lonely morning before it was time to have some lunch and then take a taxi out to the airfield.

She hadn't booked a seat, but she felt confident it would be no problem. She was terribly tempted to ring Steve and tell him she was going—thank him for— for what she didn't know. But she didn't ring him. After all, he hadn't rung her, and that in itself was a painful indication of how very little she meant to him. Not even to say goodbye—because Jan would have told him she was leaving today.

The taxi driver was chatty. Had she enjoyed her holiday? he wanted to know, and automatically she told him yes.

'Coming back to visit us again?'

'I don't think so,' she said, her smile stiff.

'Going back to the bright lights of Melbourne, I suppose.'

'That's right,' said Ellis.

At the airfield she paid her fare and he let her out and carried her bags into the small building for her, and it was not until he had driven away back to White-mark that she discovered she couldn't get a seat on the tiny six-passenger plane after all. It was full up.

It was such a complete anti-climax that Ellis was absolutely flattened. She sat down in the waiting room, her suitcases on the floor beside her, wondering if she was going to burst into tears. She longed—oh, how she longed!—to have someone there to comfort her. But there was no one. And there was only one thing she could do, and that was to go back to the hotel. She'd book a flight for the next day, and then she'd have all this—this trauma to go through again. As well, she knew she'd be struggling with herself about ringing Steve—even about going out to Warrianda. On what excuse she didn't know. But of course she couldn't possibly go, not with Jan there.

Unsteadily, she got up and went to the counter to make arrangements for the following day. She had paid for her flight and was about to ask the man behind the counter to telephone for a taxi for her when there was the squeal of brakes and a car pulled up outside. The car door flew open and a man got up and strode rapidly across the tarmac in the direction of the plane which was all ready to take off.

For a moment Ellis couldn't believe her eyes. It was Steve Gascoyne, and, completely forgetting what she had been about to say, she watched him, her heart pounding.

He was talking to the pilot now, and she wondered if he had come to see her off, to say goodbye. Half fearfully, she turned her head in the direction of his car, fully expecting Jan to be there. But the car was empty, and the next minute the door into the waiting room was flung open and he was confronting her.

Ellis felt as if she would faint at the sight of his handsome brown face, his broad shoulders looking so masterful and masculine under the wine-coloured silky shirt. His green eyes were dark with some emotion she couldn't read and they travelled over her smoulderingly, slowly, until she felt her legs ready to give way under her. Tears had sprung to her eyes and though she wanted to say something—just his name, just Steve —she was completely incapable of it.

He held out his hand to her, lean, brown, long-fingered. Unsmilingly he said, 'Ellis, come here——' and like a small child she reached out and allowed herself to be drawn to her feet.

'I—I couldn't get a seat. The plane was full,' she quavered as she went outside with him to his car, utterly submissive.

He opened the door and she slid in.

'Now you stay there, Ellis,' he said firmly. 'I'm going back for your luggage.'

Ellis sat back in the seat and let the tears run down her cheeks, though why on earth she should be crying, she didn't know. It was just seeing him again, that was all. She wept silently for a few seconds, then resolutely dried her eyes and sat up straight as she saw him coming back. She'd ask him to take her back to the hotel, explain that she was going tomorrow——

He put her suitcases in the back of the car and got into the seat beside her, but instead of starting up the motor he turned sideways and looked at her, his eyes exploring every part of her, then coming back to her lips, to her eyes.

He drew a finger along her lower lashes.

'What have you been crying for?'

Her mouth trembled slightly and she licked her upper lip, feeling it still warm because she had been weeping, and unexpectedly Steve leaned across and kissed her tenderly, quickly, his lips unfamiliarly gentle against her own.

'If you'd been on that plane, Ellis, I'd have had you unloaded,' he said, and she heard herself laugh shakily.

'Not if it had taken off!'

His dark eyebrows went up quizzically. 'If it had taken off, I'd have followed you in my own little aircraft. You wouldn't have escaped me, I promise you.'

Ellis stared at him foolishly. 'But—but why? Do you —do you want me to come back and housekeep for you and——' Her voice trailed off into silence and she looked down at her hands clasped tensely in her lap.

'You know what I want of you,' he said, then turned away from her sharply and started up the car. 'I'd better take you somewhere we can get together in privacy and talk this thing out in comfort.'

'What—thing?' she asked shakily.

'Our love affair,' he said after a second. And then, as the car got moving, she heard him say almost savagely, 'I love you, Ellis, And that's a thing I didn't mean to say till I'd got you home where you belong.'

Ellis held her breath. She must be imagining things. He couldn't have said he loved her. *He loved her!* That was what she had wanted and wanted him to say and he never had. Those were the words that would have made everything right. So why was he tossing them at her as if they were nothing—now—while they sped along the road and she couldn't even look in his eyes and see if they were true? No, she must have imagined it, she decided. He couldn't possibly love her. Besides, Jan had come back——

'I don't understand,' she said. 'Isn't Jan——' She couldn't go on, and he eased his foot off the accelerator and shot her a look that turned her limbs to jelly.

'Don't pester me, Ellis—wait till we get home, I

don't want to stop in the middle of the road and begin all that business.'

'All—what business?' she repeated, like one in a crazy dream.

'You know well enough,' he said with a sidelong glance. 'Kissing you—touching you—staking my claim ... Besides, if I stop on the road you might run away from me, and that I won't have. So shut up— because once we're at Warrianda I'm going to kiss you and kiss you until it all comes right.'

Ellis shut up. She felt utterly dumbfounded. She couldn't persuade herself she wasn't dreaming and she didn't know whether to laugh or to cry. She sat back in the seat beside him and the miles flew by until at last the shearing shed, the big hay shed, the old homestead where she had laboured came into sight, and then they were careering along the narrow white road that led to the grove of big trees that hid Steve's house.

When at last he pulled up in the drive he leaned across and opened her door for her, then they both got out and she went meekly and dazedly ahead of him into the house that she had come to love.

'In here,' he said, and took her by the upper arm and led her into the sitting room. Ellis felt his touch go through her like an electric current—tinglingly, disturbingly. With all her being she wanted to stop, to lean back against him, to have his arms come around her— to feel the warmth and the reality of him. Instead, she kept moving and then with a swift movement, he pulled her round to face him.

'Where's—Jan——' she began to ask, but her voice died away as she encountered his gaze—so intimate and so nakedly full of desire for her.

'She's not here,' he said quickly. 'I took her to join her brother in Lady Barron last night when I found her

here. I saw Martin there yesterday, when I was looking
for you. Jan told me, by the way, that you'd come for
your clothes and you'd gone on the plane yesterday.
Back to your boy-friend in Melbourne. That's why I
didn't come to Whitemark last night. I didn't discover
till I rang your uncle in Melbourne about an hour ago
that you weren't there. I got on to Whitemark then,
and that's how I found you at the airfield ... Is that
where you were going, Ellis—back to Paul?' He took
hold of her roughly and looked deeply and inescapably
into her eyes.

Ellis shook her head. 'Of course not. I was—I was
just going away——'

'Why?'

'I—I couldn't stay. You don't——'

'I don't what? What did Jan tell you?'

'That you—that everything would be all right—because she didn't want to live at Koolong any more.'

He made an impatient exclamation. 'And you believed that? Well, listen to me—I don't care where the
hell Jan wants to live. It's not going to be with me anyhow.'

'But you love her,' Ellis said in a low voice.

'I love you, Ellis,' he said, and he said it so softly and
tenderly she could have swooned. Without her even
being aware of it, he had drawn her against him and
now they sank down together on the big velvet-covered
settee, and he kissed her mouth and her eyes and then
her mouth once more, and his kiss was as sweet as
honey. It was no longer fierce and overpowering, and
it evoked no violent response from her. She felt something entirely new, something subtle and deep and
mystical, as though her mind were bewitched as well as
her body. It was as if for the first time the complete
entity that was Ellis Lincoln was meeting with the

reality that was Steve Gascoyne, and as their lips clung she seemed to taste his spirit as well as his body.

At last his mouth left hers and he murmured, 'It's all there, Ellis—all the magic of that ephemeral, incredible, impossible thing called love—a thing I thought I didn't believe in—Do I dare ask you now to marry me? I made up my mind after the cut out that I'd woo you gently, change my tactics. I was beginning to discover that something had happened to my feeling for you. You charmed me in Hobart, you know—quite against my better judgement. Then, amazingly, you were so competent around the place at Warrianda. And I did something I hadn't believed I was capable of doing and fell in love with you. But what's most incredible is that you seem to love me too ... Come here and let me taste you again—I'm not altogether sure even now that you're happy in my arms——'

'I am—oh, Steve—I am,' she murmured as she let herself be drawn back to him willingly.

'You'll marry me?' he asked at last. 'You know— when I took you to the hotel the other night, Ellis, it was for your own protection. I couldn't trust myself with you, and I didn't want you to surrender to me until I was sure you loved me. There was always some part of you that stayed so utterly aloof—so unreachable. I knew I could have your body, but I wanted so much more.'

'That's—that's how I felt,' Ellis confessed, her head against his chest. 'I guess that's really love, Steve. I couldn't give you my body unless I could believe it was more than that you wanted.'

'I do want more—I want all of you,' he said, his finger tracing the delicate line of her mouth. 'I want your sweet lips, your loving eyes—your beautiful untouched body. But I want your belief and your trust too.'

'You can have them all, Steve,' she said simply. She hesitated, then asked him anxiously, 'But—Jan——'

'Forget about Jan,' he said briefly, then seeing the troubled look in her eyes he said ruefully, 'Well, of course—I asked her to marry me. She's beautiful and healthy and she was willing, and I thought that was all I wanted. She was a—a good physical specimen to mother my children. It was as crude as that, I'm afraid. But she was greedy—and she overestimated her own desirability. She thought if she deprived me of herself she could have anything she wanted, so long as she came back.'

Ellis listened quietly, her head against his shoulder.

'I'm afraid I didn't very much care when she sent back my ring,' Steve said. 'I cared still less once you'd bewitched me ... I told you once, Ellis, that my wife could have anything she asked for—and you mentioned Koolong. Here and now I promise you that if you want to live on Koolong then we shall live there.'

Ellis caught her breath. 'No, Steve, I love it here.' She added simply, 'I'll be happy as long as I'm with you.' She didn't ask him about Patrice or Disillusion Island. Those were things he would tell her when he was ready to—in his own good time—and she was content to wait.

But about Charlie and Leanne she had to ask.

'Must they stay here, Steve?'

'What do you think, little moonbird?' His eyes exploring hers had a hint of softness and humour in them.

'I think—I think you should stop insisting,' she said after a moment. 'Let Leanne make her own decision. I think you should—believe in her love.'

'You mean you think they'll come back here?'

She nodded. 'I think she'll stick to Charlie wherever he is, if you don't—put obstacles in her way.'

Steve gathered her into his arms. 'I don't know that I want either of them back here with us, my darling. I think perhaps it's time Charlie went to Koolong and fought his own battle there. I want you all to myself at Warrianda. Would you mind very much being alone with me?'

'I'd love it,' she said, and added with a little laugh, 'After we're married, Steve!'

'Then that had better be soon,' he said vehemently, as his lips claimed hers.

The Warrender Saga

The most frequently requested series of Harlequin Romances . . . Mary Burchell's Warrender Saga

A Song Begins   The Curtain Rises
The Broken Wing   Song Cycle
Child of Music   Music of the Heart
Unbidden Melody
Remembered Serenade
When Love Is Blind

Each complete novel is set in the exciting world of
music and opera, spanning the years from the
meeting of Oscar and Anthea in *A Song Begins* to
his knighthood in *Remembered Serenade*. These
nine captivating love stories introduce you to a cast
of characters as vivid, interesting and delightful as
the glittering, exotic locations. From the tranquil
English countryside to the capitals of Europe—
London, Paris, Amsterdam—the Warrender Saga
will sweep you along in an unforgettable journey of
drama, excitement and romance.

The Warrender Saga

The most frequently requested Harlequin Romance series

Complete and mail this coupon today!

What readers say about Harlequin Romances

"Your books are the best I have ever found."
  P.B.*, Bellevue, Washington

"I enjoy them more and more
with each passing year."
  J.L., Spurlockville, West Virginia

"No matter how full and happy life might be,
it is an enchantment to sit
and read your novels."
  D.K., Willowdale, Ontario

"I firmly believe that Harlequin Romances
are perfect for anyone who wants to read
a good romance."
  C.R., Akron, Ohio

*Names available on request